DEAD RECKONING

DEAD RECKONING

BLAYNEY COLMORE

ISBN 978-0-692-30435-8

Dead Reckoning is available for bulk purchase, special
promotions, and premiums. For information on reselling
and special purchase opportunities, visit the author's
website: www.blogblayney.blogspot.com

Cover art: pastel by Lee Rich from the author's collection.
Book design by Dede Cummings / dcdesign
Brattleboro, Vermont

ACKNOWLEDGMENTS

CHARLES LINDBERGH flew from the east coast of our nation to Paris, by dead reckoning, starting at a place you know, then calculating along the way where you hope you are, that will point you where you intend. No GPS, no iPhone. Others had tried and failed, some never again heard from.

I was born before the middle of the past century to a middle class family, for whom the assumed starting point was male dominance. Several strong women provided markers points toward a new reality. Though far from wholly weaned from the old world, I am indebted to these women who gave me a good look at the world that was on its way.

Peggy, my mother, who made room in her body and her life to give me a good start.

Sylvia and Perry, my sisters, who have generously honored me even when I behaved dishonorably.

Heather, Jen and Carson, my daughters, and Louise, my step-daughter, who, in the middle of their lives, have already made the world a more humane place than they found it.

Lacey, more steadfast than mere kindness requires, for the nearly forty years of our marriage. Grateful that she has held fast even though I still can't do hospital corners.

Suzanne Kingsbury, writing guru, whose strategic, compassionate intervention at every crucial point is the only reason this book isn't on the junk pile.

Dede Cummings, whose skill pushed this book across the goal line I believed too distant to ever be reached.

AUTHOR'S NOTE

IF CELEBRATED ATHEIST Barbara Ehrenreich can own up to it, I guess I can. One cold, rainy, late fall evening in 1960, a college sophomore, I had an epiphany, a religious experience. What college sophomore in 1960 didn't? I've told almost no one about it. It's awkward to admit that it has shaped my life in the ensuing sixty-five years.

The details, now seemingly trivial, set me on the path, however meandering, I have never left.

Like many clerics, besotted by an odd career, I set out to write my memoir. I'd hardly begun when I was visited with the irresistible urge to rearrange events. And people. To turn up the volume, embellish, reveal the rich reality hidden in seemingly mundane moments.

The way a preacher would.

This is that schizophrenic, perhaps oxymoron, fiction memoir.

Those who know me will find me all over it. And, I fear, many will think they have found themselves in the story. But

I have played God, remaking events and characters to suit my fancy (a most objectionable description of God).

Biblical stories—Noah, Garden of Eden, the Battle of Jericho—didn't happen the way they're described, but they are more true than a YouTube version.

This story—an aging cleric encounters his dead mother —is meant to be true like that. Maybe not quite with biblical weight. None of this happened as I've written it, but it's all more true than anything I could write to describe what flowed from that sophomore moment.

Could be you'll find yourself in *Dead Reckoning*, the way I often find myself in stories, reconnecting with myself, repairing the connecting thread that has frayed over the decades.

That's what religion does. Religion, *ligare*—reconnect.

When Henry unexpectedly, unnervingly, reconnects with his mother, Maggie, dead twenty years, he has the choice of shutting her out, again, or reconsidering seemingly disconnected pieces of his experience, parts of himself and his world from which he had exiled himself, for fear they would be his undoing.

Henry's mind works in blank verse, not linear sequence. He occasionally breaks into verse when linear prose won't access the nuance he means to portray.

Alice, his lawyer wife—of the no-nonsense, literal, linear mind—can get testy with Henry when his language seems fuzzy, imprecise to her. She tells him she hasn't time to read his poetry, but she's secretly pleased that his work has received prizes, caused friends to treat him as a celebrated poet. She's never revealed to Henry that she keeps a paperback copy of his latest work in her desk at work.

He'd be pleased that she sometimes takes it with her to the bathroom, where, as the only woman on the firm's executive floor, she has the privacy to make it through a poem or two.

He'd be equally pleased, too, that you might do the same.

—BLAYNEY COLMORE
August 29, 2014

for Maggie

The Committee Weighs In

I tell my mother
I've won the Nobel Prize

Again? she says. Which
discipline this time?

It's a little game
we play: I pretend

I'm somebody, she
pretends she isn't dead.

—ANDREA COHEN

∽

An ounce of mother is worth a pound of clergy.
– Spanish proverb –

U P IN MY ATTIC, sorting through a decaying box packed with forty years of personal detritus, is proving more gripping than the tedious job I anticipated. Alice, my exacting wife for most of those forty years, all but pulled out my fingernails to get me to do this.

Old notes from seminary (good God, Henry, that paper on the sources of the Pentateuch belongs in a museum), a couple of citations commending my parish for housing the homeless. And tchotchkes my sisters and I couldn't bring ourselves to toss out after our mother died.

"Your mother died twenty years ago, Henry. High time." Alice said, "You're retired; all your excuses have dried up."

Thanks, Alice, for not adding, "like you."

An Episcopal parish priest for thirty years, after the order of Melchizedek (Genesis 14), probably a priest from my conception. Unlike Melchizedek, I felt at best semi-legitimate, wondered when people were going to find me out. I had a pretty good run. Rector of several fascinating parishes (every parish is fascinating in its own way), significant parishes by worldly measure, any ambitious priest would be proud of. I'm more ambitious than I'm comfortable admitting. Always feared that sullied my calling.

Early in my first term as rector (rex, regum, king, main man in Episcopal polity), I began writing poetry again, which I'd done as a boy, as an adolescent, and early in college. Poetry's built-in ambiguity seemed less hazardous than trying to make literal sense of God to an anxious congregation. All congregations are anxious in various ways; it's the mother's milk of the church.

Poetry—OK, blank verse—frees me from feeling obligated to resolve ambiguity.

Seminary and ordination looked like a respectable way to make a decent living. Mysterious ceremonies, arcane language, spiritual stealth aimed at the interior of people, a region largely uncultivated in our commercial culture.

And there was the thing about my mother, whose stuff I am sorting up here. She died an alcoholic recluse. Everything about her announced, "Leave me alone; I'm not interested in competing in this so-called civilized jungle." The "thing" about her is that I feel more kin to her than to anyone. A gifted writer, which she kept secret from most, hellaciously funny, though only a few knew. Her passion frightened her, as did any open display of her talents. She understood that brilliance arouses jealousy, competitiveness. She preferred staying hidden, drink, smoke. Nap.

Emotionally, I identify with her.

But I am a man. A brief run at using alcohol to hide myself persuaded me to choose sober, despite its attendant pitfalls. I needed a life, a legitimate life that provided a living but didn't require shutting down parts of myself I prized.

When I fell behind in school as a little boy, my mother reassured me I was normal, just fine. I was grateful, but never quite bought it. My father made it clear he thought I needed a lot of improvement. In our family his opinion counted far more than hers.

Priest seemed a hybrid solution. Respected, but acknowledged odd. My grandfather, Dad's father, was a priest, bishop, family icon. None of his sons followed him, nor understood his vocation, but they feared and respected him.

In pursuing holy orders in Episcopal Church in those days, you weren't pushed too hard about what you believed. It wasn't fatal to hold the old orthodoxies lightly.

I went for my interview with the Dean of the seminary on a bitter cold day. As I got out of my Nash Rambler, I slipped on ice. Reaching down to break my fall, I sliced open both palms on the ice. "May I help you?" the dean's secretary asked as I walked in. "I'm here for an interview," I said, holding my palms up in a gesture a priest assumes celebrating Mass, the gesture in which a million painters have portrayed Jesus. She looked at my bloody palms—my stigmata—laughed, and said, "No need for an interview, you're in."

That vocation provided welcome distance from my all-business father, yet was a vocation he respected, however begrudgingly.

Not unrelated, I married a hard-ass trial lawyer. She provided cover among parishioners, that we, too, dwelt at least partially in the real, rough and tumble world.

Dogs were important in our lives—beagles when I was a kid, Norfolk terriers after hooking up with Alice. Not only was their love dependable, they were patient, attentive listeners, a perfect foil when what I wanted to discuss with Alice, and most of the congregation, they would consider evidence I was certifiable.

Which brings me to the story I want to tell you, about my late-life (60) encounter. Though weird, it's hardly unique. Maybe loaded with clues to how we locate ourselves in the new century. How we got here, how we're coping.

It's rearranged the way I see many things.

Me? Henry Simpson. The Rev. Henry Simpson, retired cleric (ordination is an indelible stamp, not surrendered upon retirement), published poet, now house-husband, support for a busy, stressed litigator in a major law firm, and grateful companion of Gabby, a terrier who, aging as I am, has yet to let me down when I'm looking for support and a sympathetic ear.

Maybe this story is what most think—or hope—clergy tend to prior to ordination. In my experience few do, but then clergy, at least male clergy, which was the whole lot when I was coming along, lie about themselves the way men in locker rooms do, bragging about their budgets or Sunday attendance, or whatever else they hope is bigger than the other guy's. I doubt I'd ever have made even partial peace with my demons had not this story I'm about to tell you happened to me.

Maggie

ATTIC SCENE

THE WHEELS FIRST CAME OFF that languid summer afternoon up in our unfinished attic where I'd gone to do triage with that box of old papers and assorted knick-knacks my sisters and I hadn't the heart to toss out after our mother died. I'd planned to give it an hour. That was three months ago. I hadn't figured on Maggie showing up.

A little back story. About the game we humans call life.

We live our lives like a three year old with Legos, picking up randomly shaped pieces, finding where they'll connect, locking them together, sometimes despairing, sometimes delighted at the surprising shapes that emerge.

We play with differing degrees of solemnity—sometimes cynical, sometimes mischievous, sometimes desperate, sometimes self-deceiving—pretending to know how it will be shaped.

That was my beat: religion. Religio: to bind together.

In various guises, it's been my life's focus.

Thirty years, preacher, pastor, rector. If you buy the pre-packaged instructions, it's a job built on a sturdy, historical platform. The more immersed I became, the less sturdy the platform seemed.

Being a poet helps. To a poet, even something as seemingly inflexible as a creed is negotiable. A few parishioners who were wired up as I am loved having me as their rector. The larger group, who weren't, either tuned me out, worked to unseat me, or used me as the role for which priest is best suited, a canvas to project onto whatever is unresolved.

These many years later, the shape the Legos take is ever more complex, amorphous. Preaching, tending the dying, accompanying despair, administering sacraments—marriage, baptism, Eucharist—arcane, medieval remnants to most—came to seem normal to me. Maybe parishioners assume ordination provides a conduit through which the disparate pieces finally come into discernible shape.

My preaching suggested diverse ways the pieces might snap together, but the resulting shapes rarely fit expectations. Fun for a few parishioners, frustrating for many.

After thirty years, sustained by a decent pension and a high-earning wife, I stepped away from the parish to give voice to my poetry. My editor was mercifully in synch with my eccentricities. I looked forward to embracing the courage of my confusion, no longer disturbing the pious.

If You Want More

If you want
more
you better
die
because this is all there is

here.

That sort of poetry.

No search committee would have gone for it, but my publisher does. Alice, the killer litigator, thinks it's madness. She tolerates me spending my days with it only because I get paid—meagerly. It's made me a minor celebrity in our small, buttoned-down town, and leaves me free to tend things at home, if not always up to her standards.

Up here in the attic with Maggie, my mother, dead twenty years, whose DNA infested me with a unique schizophrenia—mystic cynic.

Alice will come home tonight, her energy ramped up by a day of legal combat. She'll grill me about how much culling I did of the things in this rotting cardboard box.

I was sitting on the old steamer trunk my mother's father took on his round-the-world trip when he was seventeen. Sent by his father who thought he was too young for medical school. Were it not for the Ruffles Hotel sticker, Alice would have made me get rid of it long ago. The box began to disintegrate as I pulled it open, leaving dry orange dust on my hands. Why had I let Alice bully me into this?

I was startled by something alive brushing across my hand. I nearly tipped off the trunk as I flicked a big, hairy spider off my arm, watched it scurry into a crack in the floorboards. Adrenaline rush. Heart pounding in my ears.

I reached in, my hand brushed against this miniature, midnight blue, faux–leather address/phone book. I remember it lying on her desk, next to the phone. The childlike, unimposing, tiny book matched her persona.

It fell open to V. Vest, Andrew Vest. Rector, St. Paul's, our family church in Charleston in the forties and fifties. My father a big supporter. Mr. Vest, vivid in memory. Major player in my vocation. Called himself a poor boy from Arkansas—in fact, a dandy. Tall, dressed to the nines, Brooks Brothers. Dad assumed he was born rich. Silk handkerchief in his breast pocket. Dressed like a banker, dark pin-stripe suits, but, surprisingly, his politics were leftist, radical by Charleston measure in the 1940s. He didn't mind you knowing he'd gone to Harvard Law School before seminary, practiced law, elected to a term in the Arkansas legislature. He preached about racial injustice, however veiled, anathema in Charleston then. When he laughed—he laughed way more than my parents' other friends—the wrinkles on his forehead bunched up like a bloodhound's.

I loved him.

Looking back, I'd say he was my parents' closest friend. Maybe Mom's even more than Dad's. In my thirty years as a parish priest, lots of parishioners thought I was their best friend. A potential hazard. Like Mom and Mr. Vest? What may have gone on between those two long-dead people? A couple of women probably could have derailed my clergy career. In today's church, close as Mom and Mr. Vest were, even without the fatal slip, it wouldn't fly.

"What about that, Mom? You and Mr. Vest were close; even as a kid I knew you had something going." Speaking aloud to dead people (only when no one else was around) I picked up from a Zen monk who suggested that, when escorting people from this life to the next—part of the job— you talk to them, explain why things seem strange.

"So... what about that, Henry?"

Sweet Jesus! It's close in this attic. That monk never said one of them might talk back.

"It's me, Henry—Maggie, your long-dead mother. Relax my boy, you're not coming unglued."

Like many preachers I'm an accomplished mimic, do voices. That wasn't my voice.

"Mom?" Heart thumping, I looked around, frozen in my sitting position. No clanking chains. Stuffy, still air. Humid.

"That's right, Henry, dear boy, you've summoned your old mother, Maggie, by name. Despite my intention to honor that 'eternal rest' thing."

"You lit on Andrew Vest—money shot. Twenty years dead hadn't dissipated the energy you stirred up with his name."

I got up off the trunk. Hyperventilating, short of breath. Need air. Laughter: hers. Husky, choking laugh of a lifelong smoker. Oh God. I walked in a tight little circle, stopping to look through the slatted window, orient myself. The pond was still there, reflecting the sun.

"I birthed and raised you; you're half-full of my DNA. But let's be clear. This is Maggie. Mom's dead."

Despite what some parishioners may have thought, I don't traffic with ghosts. Fact is—no offense, Maggie—do I *have* to call you that?—I find the life-after-death thing an insult to adult intelligence.

More laughter. *Her* laughter.

"Oh, you always were the earnest one, Henry; keep it within manageable bounds. I found that beguiling, even when it exasperated me. Forever rational, respectable. The spooky stuff that's always roiling inside stays under wraps. Maybe risk an occasional poem. Rational is grownup. You summoned me because you're finally ready to let those other parts of you, some of the best parts, have some air, Henry. Andrew Vest wakes up the rich things only you and Gabby talk about."

The attic hadn't heated up much yet, but I had. Beads of sweat trickled down my side. What the hell, Henry; you've listened to parishioners describe this. So you thought they were fantasizing, or nuts. Never sure, though, were you? This tiny book. Toss it out. Would please Alice. Sixty years old, Henry. You've been around the track a few times, you need this, now?

But, Andrew Vest, earliest author of my vocation. Mom's lover?

"So Mom, Maggie, how about Andrew Vest?" Am I talking to myself? "My dog was run over—I was eight—was when I took a hard left turn, first headed off the main road."

"Oh, don't I know, Henry. You may remember I was away that afternoon; it was you and Gertrude. She called Andrew."

"Right, Maggie." Practicing that name…What the hell is this? "His grip on you was as powerful as on me, wasn't it? I could tell, even as a kid, you were supercharged when he was around. Different than you usually were. You know,"—you really up for this, Henry?—"there was something about you with him, not sure how to put this, that was downright… I mean, you know, sexual."

Laughter. "And what about that, Henry, besides thinking of your mother as sexual, makes you stammer?"

"Look, Mom, Maggie, I've spent a fortune on shrinks, unpacking who you are to me. Whether you meant to, you encouraged me to give the finger to the conventional world. Dad—the sensible model for how to make it in the real world—never took center stage in me.

"And—did you know this?—I spent hours of therapy trying to figure out how women, sex, and God, got all tangled up together for me."

I was getting pissed, everything I said made her laugh.

"Make that 'Ben', Henry. Let Mom and Dad rest in their graves.

"As for your whining about not being able to untangle women, sex and God; what makes you think that makes you special? As if you hadn't signed on for that?"

My ears were ringing. Maggie, Mom, Dad, Ben, Andrew Vest, sex; I came up here to get rid of old shit, not revisit my chronic foibles. Well, Henry, you did say something about unpacking issues that still haunt you.

"OK, Ben; don't push me. Andrew got plenty of face time in my therapy. Like you. But Dad—oh shit, Ben—not that much. Tormented me. I mean, he *was* my fa-

13

ther. I figured I should stand tall, alongside him. It just never felt like a fit. You and Andrew were pretty sketchy role models. Neither of you seemed to give a damn about what mattered to most people. You flaunted your drinking, smoked wherever you pleased, made fun of the people in Charleston with major league personas—the ones Ben respected. And I got this rush, this big high, when you and Andrew did that. Even as a kid I knew that could lead to trouble."

This wasn't getting me anywhere with the box full of stuff. I'm going to tell Alice I got sidetracked by my dead mother? But I was. Bail now, Henry, or…

"So, Maggie,"—that was getting easier—"Andrew. Dad, Ben, respected him because he was scared of Graddy, Ben's father, the bishop, right? He felt bad because he thought Graddy expected him to follow him into the ministry. What a disaster that would have been. But Ben secretly thought Andrew was a leftist flake, maybe a communist, didn't he? He tolerated him, became his big supporter, because of your relationship with him. And because he hoped it might repair his guilty feelings about Graddy."

Silence. Fantasy over? Relief. All this stuff I'd skirted in therapy. I leaned down to grab a handful of papers from the box to throw out, her address book among them.

Maggie, back online.

"And all that's still hanging fire for you, Henry. No wonder you summoned me. Twenty years dead; figured I was out of reach, could rest in peace."

"*I* summoned *you*?"

That laugh again. Christ Almighty, this is nuts.

14

"Yes, Henry, *you* summoned *me*. Played on Maggie's not-yet-quite-atrophied heartstrings.

"Mother's curse, the child sprung from her loins. An electric current ran through you when you picked up that little book and it fell open to Andrew. Kinetic energy roused me from a place I considered settled. Oh, my dear boy, I should have burned the book before I died."

How long had I been up here? The sun had moved to the other side of the house, the half-moon window now in shadow. Chilly. Alice would be home soon. The chickadees were making their last call before dark. Cut to the chase, Henry. Courage. Breathe.

"OK, Maggie. Did you and Andrew Vest have an affair?"

Sigh. A shrink told me when his patient sighs he pays attention; she's about to cough up something big, buried way deep.

"Oh, Henry, such heavy baggage you're lugging around. What are you remembering about Andrew?"

A kaleidoscope of memories.

"That time Eisenhower held a telethon in Charleston. You and Andrew thought he'd take a question from a child. And he did. You had me ask why he didn't repudiate Joseph McCarthy. I hadn't the faintest idea what that meant, but I loved being in on something I sensed was subversive in our southern, Republican town.

"I knew not to mention it to Dad—Ben. I've never forgotten it. Felt like being admitted to a secret society.

"And the day Gertrude scraped Birdie's guts off the road. Andrew came right over, spent the whole afternoon with Gertie and me. I've always loved him for that."

"So have I, Henry."

"In clergy workshops, when we were asked to describe a childhood moment that started us on the road to ordination, I wrote about Andrew and Birdie and Gertrude that afternoon. I didn't admit that you popped up, alongside Andrew, but you did."

I choked up. Get a grip, man. That was more than fifty years ago. Getting dark. Alice'll drive in any minute. Cut it short.

"So, Maggie, can we just get through this one thing; *did* you have an affair with Andrew?"

Heavy silence.

"Did *you*, Henry?"

The crunch of wheels on the driveway. I Hadn't pulled a single scrap out of that box. Best grab a handful before I go downstairs and face Alice.

꙳

There are many paths to ordination in the Episcopal Church. One, model yourself after those who absorb the workings of the institution, who succeed in the sense a CEO in business succeeds. Bishops, cardinal rectors, bureaucrats. Another, walk a tightrope, take a flier on a separate reality. Maybe even try it on a little for yourself.

I suppose I straddled those two. Alice humors my balancing act, doesn't consider it of great moment. A talented, aggressive litigator, she holds to a fiercely singular reality, finds my dithering a lunacy only my peculiar vocation would tolerate.

Not until late middle age did I reluctantly admit to myself that it was my mother, our family's Rodney Dangerfield (I didn't get no respect), who had the strongest claim on my psyche, shaping my choices. Not something I wished to broadcast. By every conventional measure, she was pretty much a ne'er do well. Or *was* she, Henry? So far, in this second act, she seems pretty different.

You couldn't invent a more apt place to visit a ghost than our attic, thick with spider webs, raw beams, rusty roofing nails that can tear a hole in your scalp if you forget to duck. Mouse infested. I dispatched thirty mice last fall.

Maggie. Dead twenty years, wasted by alcohol. Her death as much relief as grief, to her and to us. It's not as if she hasn't haunted me before, though not quite so audibly. Maggie had seemed content to let the world go by without her, agoraphobic, alcoholic. But she's hung around me all my life. Especially as I was trying to work out what it was to be a so-called holy man, shaman. She and her co-conspirators—lovers?—Andrew Vest, one or two others, doing that different-drummer thing, made my juices run. I wanted so much to fit that into being priest without making myself an outcast.

This farmhouse is old–1830. Alice and I love old things, just not the *same* old things. Despite fancying myself a leftist—socialist, if you ask my parishioners—I'm a closet medievalist. Old masters, archaic liturgy, Elizabethan language.

Alice loves antiques, early American furniture, houses built before 1850. I like old houses better than flimsy contemporary construction, but cracked plaster, weakened floorboards, easy access to mice, leaking rainwater, and money, not so much.

Alice fell in love with this place first time we saw it. We looked at newer, tighter houses, with updated plumbing and wiring. Alice thought they lacked patina.

This attic, two hundred years of patina that Alice never sees. Talk about patina—how about Maggie, my moldering mother?

Up here with the mice and spiders, combing through these boxes, dripping patina I'd just as soon skip. I promised Alice. It is tranquil. And hospitable to at least one ghost I never intended to court. You catch a glimpse of the pond through the latticed half-moon window under the eave, a reminder that the world's still out there. Geese serenade in 24-hour cacophony. The beaver swims down to our end at dusk most afternoons in search of new sprouts. For all my complaining, I quite like it up here. Spooky, like a monastic chapel. I can lose myself in other-worldly reverie. I sometimes imagine I could have lived a cloistered, monastic life had I been less attached to worldly ease.

And to being married. Alice contrasts herself with me, says she's grounded in reality. *Her* reality, I used to insist, before I learned the futility of debating a litigator.

This morning Alice, having her power breakfast standing by the refrigerator, spooning yogurt from the carton, decked out in pin-stripe, full-lawyer persona. "Henry, you've been promising for years to go through the junk in those boxes. Get to it, or I'm going to toss the whole mess out. Your mother's been dead twenty years.

"I mean, seriously, your mother's detritus is bad enough,

but forty-year-old seminary notes? Sermons no one listened to at the time. I mean it, Henry, the rate you're going, all that crap is going to be left for some cleaning service after we die."

As I was mentally composing a response—especially to that offensive *sermons no one listened to at the time* crap, Alice rinsed her spoon, picked up her briefcase, gave me a perfunctory kiss, a last command—"I know you'll make a dent in that junk by the time I get home"—and was out the door, car started, garage door raised, lowered, tires crunching gravel.

I can't keep pace with Alice. I mostly quell my petulance at her scalding, parent-voice that rouses my latent adolescent I've tried, and failed, to subdue my entire adult life.

I have to admit she's right about this; it's overdue. Exorcise Mom's ghost. And maybe a few others along the way.

I still sometimes accuse myself of having backed into ordination. Since I stepped down from preaching, I've become kinder to myself, can affirm how I got there. It was like sleep-walking. The biggest surprise came years afterward, well along the path to success in the CEO model—rector of what's called a Cardinal parish—I began getting weary with maintaining the institution, edging closer to that slippery slope, down which lies murky mystery.

More than anything, tending to the dying fed my passion for priest's work. It probably kept me going several years longer than I might have otherwise. That and getting vested in the pension fund.

Alice told people I was death obsessed. I spent a lot of time with dying people, more than the job required. Hanging out with people who knew they were dying, the cultural pretentions, illusions, peeled away, gave me weird energy. Akin to sexual energy. Almost made up for the posturing required for dealing with the money guys and church bureaucrats.

Hard to admit that ordination was a way to avoid the world of business. Ironically, the larger the church, the more it was like any business. My father, Ben, a moderately successful businessman, worried I was too much like Maggie, couldn't do what was required of a man in the world. I worried about that, too. Then worried that I had been co-opted by big, rich parishes.

Retiring softened that anxiety, but I can't say it altogether found a happy place for whatever it was Andrew Vest and a few others awakened in me.

A decade into parish priest, I embraced the reality (with some help from therapists) that my vocation and Maggie were intertwined. Even a devout Freudian would find that hackneyed. I told myself (and the bishop) that I'd had a more varied, elegant call from God. Figured Andrew and Birdie would play better than Maggie. I think I did have a real calling, just not exactly the kind people understand.

Maggie's part remains elusive. And undeniable.

The musty attic with my dead mother's artifacts seems the right place for revisiting how she impacted my life. Out in the world, exposed to oxygen, it's still flammable, threatens to make me the self-immolating outlier Maggie considered herself.

It was a welcome moment for me when Alice finally took Maggie for who she was, stopped clucking about her addictions and failings. Alice knows it makes me uncomfortable, considering how much Maggie there is in me.

Maggie and Alice reached a civil, begrudging, mutual respect, but Maggie never made sense to Alice, nor Alice to her. Alice, prize litigator—first woman in that role at Armstrong, Bucks, Jervis & Riggs. Parishioners joked about the rector's wife being a kick-ass lawyer, balancing the bleeding-heart rector.

The year before we married, at breakfast with Maggie at her old, metal-top, kitchen table (Ben gone by then, on to his mid-life adventure), I told her Alice and I were getting married. She was hung over, as usual, in her tired, green, flannel bathrobe, hair askew, smoker's hack. She didn't react. Had she heard me? Her favorite trick, looking vague, out of it. Staring at me, vacantly. You in there, Mom?

"You sure you're up for marrying Alice, Henry? She's not as bright as you are, hasn't much interest in that business you call the inner life. A little wanting for humor. She has an unexamined, conventional belief in God for which you have no patience. But I'll give her this: she's street-smart, ten times tougher than you, better equipped for real life. You know, Henry, come to think of it, maybe she's exactly what you need in a wife."

Maggie's pitiless insight. Just when you thought she had checked out, zap! The memory of that conversation has stayed with me.

She had it right. Venus and Mars doesn't touch it. Alice and I are fire and water. Parishioners bragged that we weren't afraid for them to see us fight. We tried to keep our bloodiest battles for home. I suppose we challenged the stereotype of vapid clergy couples. I'd just as soon conflict wasn't quite such a hallmark of our marriage.

I've never been sorry I married Alice. Well, maybe not never. Being married to her remains my greatest adventure. Marriage, at least ours, if it isn't stillborn, is an endless, unfinished experiment. I fell in love with several other women, before and after we were married, but I knew better—even when my libido trumped my judgment—than to think I could have made a lasting alliance with any of them. Or that life with any of them would have been half the adventure life with Alice is every day.

Alice helped curb my lusting after other women. When the therapist in our prenuptial counseling asked us what we expected of each other, Alice, without so much as a smile, said, "Oh Henry can do whatever he likes, so long as he doesn't mind having his balls shot off."

⌁

I composed this poem one Ash Wednesday, preparing to impose ashes on penitents' foreheads, and I'd hoped would work for the homily that day. Too provocative for church, but my editor loved it. A lot of old, bottled-up stuff got released as I edited my poetry for the book. I received a modest advance. The editor had been on the vestry of my last parish. She broke her resolution against advances, probably out of pity. (You couldn't bring yourself to think she might like your work, and it might sell, could you, Henry?).

Much of the poetry in the book will be pieces I chickened out of using as a sermon.

Lent 2K

I

I saw my first ashes
Robert's "cremains"
in November 1966.

I'd known the
guy a
little. Startled me. Thought
I could identify a knuckle or
maybe
the round piece that hinges the elbow. I
broke that one playing
football
when I was 9.

"They're like the
ashes
you spread on roses," the undertaker said.
Not these. They're bones
parts of
Robert I think I can make
out.

II

Then there was

Ossie's
ashes.

Last time I saw Ossie
intact he
was in intensive
care. "Unresponsive," so
the nurse said.
I whispered into his ear,
"Ossie, it's me,
Henry."

His brow
furrowed, head shifted
one eye opened a narrow
slit
pupil fixed, staring straight
ahead.

"You need to take down those
goddamn
trees beside your house,"
Ossie said, clear as
that, "they've grown too tall."

Last words. A week
later
on a tug off Martha's
Vineyard with Ossie's widow and four
big sons, all in oilskin

souwesters, driving, slanting, stinging rain,
blowing like
stink
we tossed Ossie's ashes overboard
just
as the wind shifted and
we all inhaled a little of
Ossie.

III

Remember O
wo/man
dust thou
art.

Fat Tuesday night we sang
"Carne vale." The
flesh
fled our bones,
our bones
burned to
ash
mingled
with the dirt and
disappeared to
dust.

Good News.

In the past 35
years
they've radically upgraded our
cremains
crushing them to fine
powder. No more
knuckles and no less
dead.

Never ran that one by Alice. She can read it when the book comes out. Probably won't.

⤳

Determined to get rid of stuff in the box, not let the Maggie séance eclipse the reason I came up to the attic in the first place. This morning I bypassed Maggie's book, pulled an envelope out of the box. Battle decorations won by Maggie's cousin, Ramon de Murias, in WWII. As a kid I prized those. Throw them out? Sacrilege. How come Maggie had them, not Ramon's family? I put the envelope on the rough floor board. Maggie was a de Murias before she was a Simpson. That makes me something like one quarter de Murias: Cuban. Maggie's mother came from Cuba.

Always wondered about that Latin blood. Henry, you and Alice are going to come a cropper if you keep getting sidetracked up here.

Speaking of Alice, better get downstairs, get moving on supper, feed and walk Gabby. Damn, life keeps getting in the way.

And there's this Maggie business.

"I'll be back, Maggie. Need to tend to business. Hope you don't mind my keeping you waiting."

Big sigh. Maggie's sigh, so familiar, but so long ago. Or was that *my* sigh? Get real Henry, of course it's yours. Don't start getting all spooky in your old age. I put Maggie's book on top of the box, picked up Ramon's war decorations. Ramon de Murias, the Cuba connection. My DNA has more moving parts than I remember anyone in our family ever talking about.

Toss out Ramon's war medals? Alice would. I put them back in the box, looked longingly at Maggie's book, and headed downstairs, empty-handed, to face lawyer Alice.

Alice & Henry Contend

ALICE NEVER JUST WALKS into the house; she makes an entrance. Bulging briefcase, oversize pocketbook, her basket heavy with whatever she's fancied at Trader Joe's on her way home. Usually on her Bluetooth, still negotiating as she comes through the door. I never get it, always think she's talking to me. I respond, inappropriately, to something I misheard, drawing an annoyed look and a signal to keep quiet.

Alice and I have nervous systems that navigate the world at different velocities.

Today she's not on her Bluetooth. She bursts through the door from the garage, breathless, as if she'd run all the way home, and fires a question about something for dinner she's been hoping—expecting—she assumes I've been preparing.

"Henry," (decibels high, she hasn't sighted me yet) "did you clean out that box in the attic? Have you peeled the potatoes? I thought we'd have potato salad along with the piece of fish I got at Trader Joe's."

I've learned the futility of responding too quickly. In her haste to unload her armful, check phone messages, take a lap through the mail, she has moved on from her own question. She'll return to it without warning, when I will have forgotten it.

My strategy is to look busy, begin peeling potatoes (who knew that's what we were having? I'd planned pot stickers). I was glad for a moment to think up a response about why I didn't get rid of any of the things in the box, whenever we got back to that. I was feeling squeamish about having failed that test. After completing her rounds, Alice returned to the kitchen, fixing me with her lawyer stare.

"Well, what about that box?"

"How about a hello, and maybe some semblance of a welcome-home kiss?" (Buy time, Henry.)

"Oh, sorry Henry."

Nice kiss, lingered a little, compensation for having brushed hurriedly by me. Once her entrance would have made me resentful. Over the years it's become a cat and mouse game I quite enjoy. I try to seduce her into a kiss with less hurried, soft lips, one of the ways to detour her litigator persona, steal into her less guarded place. My courage to come clean about the neglected box was boosted by that warm kiss.

"I'm hopeless, Alice. First thing I pulled out was my mother's ridiculous little address/phone book that sat on her desk when I was a kid. I opened it at random, right to the name of the guy who was our rector in Charleston, the guy I've told you about, who played such a big part in my going to seminary."

I was over the sink peeling potatoes; Alice was pulling things out of the fridge, looking for the open bottle of Chardonnay. Our derrieres brushed, our eyes on our separate tasks, not each other. Made my confession feel less risky.

"As I thought about that guy, I had this really strong sense that he and my mother may have had an affair. And right there the cleaning-out project got sidelined."

Alice's explosive laugh startled me. In a way it was a relief. The stuff about Andrew Vest and my mother hadn't struck me as particularly funny, but that was probably a helpful way to think about it. It was, after all, more than fifty years ago. A little precious to find it traumatizing now.

"No wonder you became a parish priest, Henry, being privy to the secret lives of all those restless women, women like your mother. Oh Sigmund Freud, blow your trumpet!"

Alice's teasing could feel cruel; the cross-examiner in her was forever alert to an opening to probe a tender spot. I smiled, I can take the joke, even at my expense. I've trained myself to see Alice's humor as antidote to my chronic heaviness, my tendency to consider my insights divine revelation. Alice found the wine, was working at extracting the cork I'd jammed in the night before.

"Let me give you a hand with that," I said, taking the bottle from her, working the cork free. Not exactly rescuing her from a saber-toothed lion, but a welcome chance to show my man-strength. Fed my courage to challenge her teasing.

"Well, no doubt the motives of people who get ordained are as complex as those who join the bar." I knew it was feckless to trade jabs with skilled-litigator-Alice, but I thought I'd parried her thrust pretty neatly.

Alice poured herself a glass of the chardonnay. "Maybe, Henry," she said, her tone flat, "but when we decide to become a lawyer, we don't claim it was God's idea."

Hang it up, Henry. This is your garden-variety power-struggle, not metaphysics. Best drop it. Move on.

"I also came across an envelope that held her cousin Ramon de Murias' war medals. Why'd she have those rather than someone in his own family? She and Ramon were close, more like brother and sister than cousins. She'd hinted that Ramon was a war hero, but I'd forgotten about the medals. Impressive. Some of that stuff is going to be hard to toss out."

As I was mid-sentence Alice disappeared around the corner into the pantry. I paused, felt foolish talking to empty space.

"Keep talking, Henry, I'm just getting some onions." Conversations with Alice require following her from room to room, the way Gabby follows us. Irritates me, tempts me to say something petulant. In therapy we'd discussed my learning to shrug these moments off so they wouldn't end up derailing us.

"No doubt there's plenty in that box to distract you, Henry—distraction is your middle name—but did you manage to get rid of *any* of it?"

"I actually sorted through quite a bit," I lied, "and made a good start at culling the rest."

Alice's laugh was sarcastic. "Did you actually throw out *anything*, Henry?"

"Look, Alice, I know you're eager for me to get rid of that box; so am I. But I'm having an encounter with my mother that's knocking me off my pins. More affecting than any I had when she was alive."

Finally we were eyeball to eyeball. Alice, quizzical, silent, considering her response.

"You know, Henry, if whatever you mean by 'encounter' could help you make peace with the way your mother has haunted you for as long as I've known you, I could almost forgive you for futzing around up there instead of getting on with what you went up there to do."

That came out of left field. *Haunted*? It wasn't delivered with the scolding tone I might have expected. Alice, wine glass in hand, studied me intently. Unnerving the way she could suddenly focus, so totally. *Haunted*?

"You've never said anything about my being haunted by my mother."

"Haven't I? Never said anything about her drinking and passivity, her agoraphobia you and your sisters worry might have shaped your lives? Come on, Henry, you've all but admitted that getting ordained was an attempt to balance yourself between your over-achieving father and your passive mother."

That stung. It's true I had admitted something like that to Alice, in an unguarded moment, trusting her with something I knew she could use as a weapon. My motive for being ordained? OK, maybe partly to buy off my parents, but hardly the whole story. And who said it was, Henry? Tender spot, swallow, breathe.

Neither of us noticed the water for the potatoes come to a boil. The dog was jumping up on us, first Alice, then me, the way he did when he sensed we were on the cusp of something that might end in grief, raised voices. Gabby hates conflict. That's my dog.

"You know, Henry, I think your sisters envied you that choice. If the church had ordained women thirty years ago, Jean might have done the same thing. Victoria's probably too hard-headed, like me."

Where had this been all these years?

"So Alice, suppose I told you that the mother I met in the attic today wasn't that passive sot who always bugged me, but a force, a woman to be reckoned with?"

Alice didn't hesitate. "I'd say you finally met the woman I knew the moment I met her, but you never seemed to."

I turned to the stove just as the water began to boil over, yanked the pot off the burner. Alice's tone, delivering that biting insight, was gentle, not accusing. It still stung.

"So you're telling me I've had my mother wrong all these years. And you, who only knew her for a short time before she died, knew her better?" That was a little defensive, Henry.

"No, Henry," Alice took a step closer, put her palm on my cheek, unusual gesture, "I don't for one minute think I knew your mother better than you did. Differently. I wasn't her son, wasn't desperate for her approval. Which is a good thing, because I never got it."

That broke the ice. Alice put her arms around me. We hugged and laughed. The tension evaporated. Alice finished her glass of wine and I poured her another half a glass. Disciplined Alice never allowed herself more than a glass and a half. I poured myself a beer, sautéed the flounder, sliced and buttered the potatoes. She fixed a green salad.

Over dinner I learned more about her client who she

believed had been set up by his own company and by the CIA. Alice had a full head of steam about it, thrilled that it looked like her partners thought she had heavy enough weapons to handle the case on her own. Her client should be too. I'd sure want her on my side. I was happy that it eclipsed her monitoring my progress in the attic. Tomorrow's a new day.

The attic encounters, Alice's comments about Maggie and my vocation, reignited issues I once thought had cooled. Guess not. My old embarrassment, feeling I'm Maggie's heir, our family closet case, in too many ways. Sometimes I feel as if I designed my whole life to compensate. Chronic worry, Henry.

⤳

Gabby and I had an exhilarating outing after breakfast. I'd given up running a decade earlier, but when Gabby pulled on his leash on crisp mornings like this, I'd do a short jog, clear out the cobwebs. Even worked up a mild sweat, releasing endorphins, the sense of well-being welcome antidote to fretting over the world's, and my own, misfiring.

Gabby gobbled his come-home treat and climbed onto his monogrammed cushion. Nothing too good for our boy. I climbed the attic stairs. Does Gabby dream of running free? I wondered if my Maggie encounter was a day dream, maybe a ghost encounter. Last night I dreamed Maggie was reading a New Yorker poem to me. Wished I could remember it. Might work in the collection I promised my editor I'd get to her before year's end. My poetry, which Alice finds just this side of madness, turns my wondering to fascination, a sanity saver for me.

Back to the attic. Open the box, pull out Maggie's book.

"You know what I've been thinking, Henry?"

No preliminaries. Maggie, full sprint, right out of the starting blocks.

"No, Maggie, I don't. I'm all ears."

"Oh, that's my boy," she laughed. I wished I could see her. So few of my memories of her were light-hearted, but her laugh was; made me happy to hear it again. "Your professional life spanned tidal shifts in many areas, none more than the slippery business of gender roles. In the church and the world. Too late for me, though I can't say I would have chosen to play in that heavy traffic anyway.

"At the start of your career you male clergy worked hard to at least look manly. Of course, not only were many secretly gay, but there's a strong feminine caste to the role. Pretty schizophrenic. And you had an added dimension—me. I knew you were perplexed that you thought you were wired like me, and I seemed to have dropped out of the world you still had to navigate.

"You're too tough on yourself about that, Henry. You figured out how to use what you got from me and make it work pretty damn nicely. You're too reluctant to focus on so much of your life that was terrific. Some because you were smarter and braver than you've ever let yourself believe.

"I'm going to give you a look at a moment you probably have forgotten. Hard to believe what you're about to watch was in the early '70s, more than forty years ago. I wonder if you knew how you unnerved those guys."

Maggie had me all tuned up. Look! There I am, done up in clerical collar, gray shirt, khakis, tweed sport coat, standard uniform for preppy clergy in New England. I know that meeting room. St. Paul's Cathedral in Boston. Forty years later, still familiar. And those guys vivid in memory.

Twenty men seated in a circle. No need to count. It's a meeting of the Twenty Club, twenty rectors of the largest and—so we told ourselves—most significant Episcopal churches in the Boston area. We met once a month over lunch. One of us would deliver a paper.

Twenty men, aged thirty-five to eighty, half in clerical collars, half in tweed and bow ties. My day to deliver. Forty years later I heard the anxiety in my voice as I cleared my throat and began to speak. Sometimes members spoke off the cuff, but my subject was too sensitive to think I could keep my cool without a manuscript.

Much more obvious now than then, how disinterested they looked, anticipating another posturing paper, meant to impress, about which they could care less. Tough audience, full of lobster Newburgh, a couple of glasses of wine. I remember being unsure this was a good idea. Hoped they'd sleep through it.

"You ready, Henry?" Maggie asked, chuckling. "You're futzing around, stalling as much now as you did then."

Before I could respond, I heard my own voice. Any sense of being in my attic was gone. I was in that room in the cathedral.

"I wonder how many of you have ever heard of the Zuni man-woman?" I began. Christ, Henry! Might have paused here. Too nervous. "There is a people from the region, now

New Mexico, among whom a few with a special role, man/woman, carry the identity of both genders, neither exclusively. They are revered, considered holy. Healers, soothsayers, keepers of sacred ceremony, responsible for esoteric functions. Healing, interpreting dreams, doing exorcisms. They are exempt from the work the rest of the tribe does."

A couple of the men looked up from their near nap, their expression suggested they saw what was coming.

"We clergy, a pretty weird guild in this culture, tolerated, even in many ways honored, by crusty Yankees whose tight boundaries exclude them from whatever it is they imagine we may be up to. It makes us uncomfortable, but we're used to being marginal, and, truth be told, we rather enjoy being different, special."

I was gaining confidence; several of them perked up.

"Well, my brothers, as I was reading about these people, it occurred to me that *we* are sort of like those Zuni men/women. What if we took a leaf from their book? Inadvertently, we have a unique offering to make to our culture, as it goes through wrenching, confusing issues about gender."

I'd paused, to breathe, gather courage to go on, could see this was penetrating their postprandial slumber. Their eyes now riveted on me, even old Jack Crocker's, the oldest, who always slept through the presentation.

"Look, most people already think we're strange, and let's face it, we are. We dress up in ancient costumes that look more like women's dress today—so do the Zuni men/women—conduct arcane ceremonies which, if anyone ever did understand, no one—including us—does any longer."

Another pause. Several of them edged forward in their

chairs. The waiters finished clearing the table, no more rattling dishes. Coffee had been served but I didn't see anyone sipping theirs.

"We are authority figures in our communities, but our authority is unlike the authority carried by other men, business and political leaders. We spend more time with women than the other men do. Those women tell us secrets they don't tell their husbands, one reason the men fear and hate us, and are reluctant to challenge our authority."

The tension in the room is palpable. I can smell the man odor, as if we were in a locker room. I'd forgotten Maggie, the attic, everything except getting through this paper.

"I hope I'm not offending anyone when I say it's common knowledge that ordination in the Episcopal Church has always attracted more than our share of homosexuals (gay wasn't then in common use). It may still be risky to come out of the closet in most parishes, but smart people don't miss that reality."

This is close to the bone (apt metaphor). One guy in the group had come out to me privately, and I was pretty sure a couple of others were, too. Clergy get good at looking unruffled by scary stuff. It's a survival thing. If any of them were freaking out, I couldn't read it.

"If you're remotely like me, you harbor the wish there was something useful you had to offer, something tangible, unlike the mostly nebulous way we spend our days. Whether you're a particularly manly man or not, you're always aware you're never quite one of the guys.

"What if we were to sponsor ourselves as the WASP equivalent of the Zuni man/woman? Declare ourselves, neither distinctly male nor female, but both? And neither?"

Lots of shifting in chairs and checking watches. My twenty minutes presenting to the Twenty Club are nearly up.

"Yes, I know most of you are married, like me. So are the Zuni men-women. Seems to me the issue isn't whether we fit the identity our culture assigns to men—especially men at the top of the food chain—but that our culture has exhausted the traditional gender definitions, and is having a hellish hard time working out where to go from here.

"Particularly men. Gloria Steinem has provided some new possibilities for women, but who's stepping up for men?"

OK, Henry, don't wimp out. You've put it out ther. Finish with a flourish.

"I think it's pretty interesting to wonder what it would be like to declare ourselves some version of the Zuni man/woman in a Boston Brahmin context"—now, there's a reach, Henry—"as a sacrificial offering to a perplexed culture."

"Thanks for listening. I'm glad to stick around and talk with anyone who's interested."

Polite applause. More looking at watches, shuffling of chairs, mumbling about meetings, hospital visits, as they gather their things and file out, most without saying anything or making eye contact.

Except old Jack Crocker, retired Headmaster of Groton School, the oldest, closest the Twenty Club has to a living legend. Jack waits until all the others have left, then comes up to me. He's stooped, a few remnants of his lunch on his rep tie. He puts his hand on my shoulder, his eyes look directly into mine.

"Henry, that was fascinating, provocative, brilliant. Just when I'd given up hoping there might be some innovative possibility for rescuing Episcopal clergy from our well-deserved oblivion. You know, ever since my old school began taking girls, I hear from faculty that gender identity is the most challenging issue they face with the kids. I'm too old to absorb all this, but it's a big deal, and it's not going away.

"I can't thank you enough for this. I'd be eager to find a time to talk further. If you could give me the title of that book, I'd like to read it. But right now I've put off a trip to the bathroom perilously long for a man my age, so I must excuse myself."

I'd been so caught up that I was startled when Maggie and the attic come back into focus.

"How does that grab you, Henry?" she asked.

"Well, holy shit, Maggie, pretty heartening. Funny, I don't think I understood then half what I see in it now. I'd love to go back and give the talk again, in a hundred different places. Brilliant, insightful, if I do say so.

"I can't remember now whether I had another chance to talk with Jack Crocker."

"He died less than a month after that meeting," Maggie said. "Great he was there that day. Even all these years later, you can feel what it was like having everyone except Jack Crocker run off. I wonder how long it took you to see how revolutionary, far-seeing, how brave you were to give that talk to those guys?"

"Until now, Maggie."

⌒

I took a couple of days off to process that session.

I discovered if I left Maggie's book untouched, Maggie didn't show. Then I could sort through—throw out—things that weren't emotionally charged. Reassure Alice—and myself—that I was actually doing what Alice considered the purpose of my being in the attic.

I spent a few hours at my desk editing poetry I'd promised my editor a month ago. I shouldn't have accepted an advance. My conscience suffered from parking overtime on her dime. Composing poetry kept me grounded in that alternate reality, gave me confidence to continue the Maggie encounters without trying to make sense of what they were.

I'd been commissioned to compose a poem to mark the centennial of the library in a small Vermont town, far from the literary mainstream. Probably wouldn't improve my chances for a Pulitzer. My editor loved the angle, which she thought might provide a marketing possibility.

Ex nihilo
An ode to the Moore Free Library
On its Centennial

He borrowed his words with care
Hungry to create
not merely emulate
while
Standing onshore

breathing unfiltered
air.

Six times before, he'd ventured here
partnering with God
the works of creation
while Noah's passengers looked on
bemused.

Now he's certain he's gained his legs
and
can stomp the slithering serpent
into
submission.

"Let us make one like us,"
the lesser gods slyly
tempted
God
Who thought it great sport to fashion a
speaking, reading, writing
beast
who, despite these impressive tricks was
nonetheless
beast.

Now your library
among the artifacts of the period

called
Homo Erectus
(sapiens no longer)
stands
Witness to the brief geologic moment
in which
the weights and measures of physics
the forces of gravity and brevity
were thought to have been
repealed.

Creation Crowns
itself each aeon
with some One who fancies herself
central
irreplaceable
immortal
Divine.

This time the
Word made flesh
was It.

Your multi volume temple
protruding proudly
through
spider webbed
roach infested
worm aerated
forest,

speaks silently of
what
Was in the beginning
is now And will be
Forever.

I wrote that before there was an internet. Or Facebook or Twitter. Zuni Man/Woman, the world beyond print, maybe I am a prophet? May God spare me.

Poetry works better for me than therapy. It's my form of meditation. Maggie and her book were crowding almost everything else out at the moment. Welcome distraction, a poem to revise.

Terry Robinson

I SO WANTED TO ASK MAGGIE about a name in her book, entered in a different way from the others, in a different place, in an unfamiliar hand.

Seated myself on the steamer trunk, shifting my weight, searching for a position kind to my sciatic.

On the book's title page, the name was scribbled in what looked like a child's scrawl.

"Terry Robinson?" I asked. "I think that's the name. One of the few I don't recognize. Not your handwriting, on the title page rather than under the R tab. Who is Terry Robinson, Maggie?"

"Terry Robinson wrote her name there herself. I bet you remember her, that little girl I began tutoring in reading when she was seven years old. Terry Robinson was white, but lived on the edge of the Charleston ghetto. Google her sometime. Fascinating story. Her life had many chapters, from drug addicted prostitute to celebrated author. I was privy to most of them. Among my most treasured relationships. If she were still around you'd love her too. In fact you met her. You'll remember as we get into her story.

"What I suspected about her when I first knew her as a child became unmistakable as she entered adolescence. Terry was born a boy. A hermaphrodite actually, but in Britain, where she was born, the law said she was male. Very bright, sweet. I wondered if he might be what's now called gay. But something about that didn't seem to quite fit. We think a seven year old doesn't yet have a fully formed gender identity. Maybe not, but something about Terry made me suspect, even then, he was more she than he."

"Like?"

"Like how it made me feel to be with her."

"How she made you feel? A *seven* year old?"

"Don't start with that scolding, shaming clergy voice, Henry. It doesn't become you. Weirder than Zuni man/woman? I know; these days everyone's jumpy about sexual predators. Terry wrote his name in the front of that little book the day he gave it to me. I'm pretty sure he stole it from the drug store. He was eleven then. I had been tutoring him for four years. We were reading Truman Capote's *In Cold Blood.*"

No wonder it looks like a kid's writing; it was.

"You were reading *In Cold Blood* with an *eleven* year old?"

"Kill the shaming voice, Henry. Shame has no currency with me, and it doesn't become you. Yes, I was reading *In Cold Blood* with Terry, who happened to be eleven at the time, a very mature eleven. From the moment I met her—him, then— I found it impossible to ignore. I couldn't quite make it out, but it was powerful. He set those brown eyes on me as if they saw, not just into my soul, but deeper… way down, right into my sex."

"Your *sex*, Maggie? You mean gender, or fucking? Apologies for being crude."

"No need for games, Henry; you understand well enough. Sorry to make you uncomfortable. Your old mother stirred up like that, by a transgender child. Shall we revisit the Twenty Club?"

Maggie's sputtering, choking laugh. The fun of it hadn't hit me yet. This must have been how some of those guys in the Twenty Club felt that day.

"Just being with her woke wonderful, woman energy in me, energy I had trained myself to keep quiet. It was uncomfortable, I'll tell you. Remember, she was eleven, and I wasn't. And she was still theoretically a boy, though her feminine energy eclipsed her maleness. I had no particular interest in young boys. Except of course for you, Henry."

Maggie laughed at her own joke. At my expense? You're sensitive today, Henry.

"Got it, Maggie. So you're telling me you were gay? I mean why not get the big secrets out there right away?"

This evoked a scornful laugh.

"Come off it. Henry. No need to wedge what makes you uncomfortable into some tight little container so you can give it a name and dismiss it. I'm not telling you anything, except the way my body, my affect and intellect, my whole being responded to being with Terry. If it's of any comfort, nothing about that powerful feeling resulted in more than deep affection and respect. I trusted my body's responses, didn't fret that it might erupt into what is now labeled inappropriate behavior. Terry's maleness just was unconvincing, like a role she'd been assigned and was ready to shed. When she was fifteen she read about the gender clinic at Johns Hopkins. She asked me if I knew anything about it."

Johns Hopkins! Wait a minute. There's a name in Maggie's book I'm pretty sure connects with Johns Hopkins.

"Oh my God, Maggie. Click! I guess you knew a little something about Johns Hopkins. Takes us to the Ds in your address book. David Daniels. Lucky break for Terry that you and Dr. Daniels were such *special* friends." What's with the sarcasm, Henry?

"Well, good for you, Henry. For someone still in the fog of the quick, you're downright prescient. Want to tell me what you think you know about David Daniels?"

Despite what I suspected about Johns Hopkins and David Daniels, I deserved her scorn. My aunt, Maggie's sister, had told me about Maggie and Ben's early married days, living next door to another young couple with whom they became intimate. Spouse-swapping? In the 1930s? Who knew? Prurient possibility. Those photos of the four of them, looking like a commune. Why should that do a number on me? My lower back, sciatic, my stress-places, ached.

"You hitting the wall, Henry?"

Unnerving how Maggie could read me. Could when she was alive. And we considered her out to lunch? No wonder my sisters and I tried to hide from her whatever in us made us jumpy. Never worked. She always knew.

"I do feel a little done-in, Maggie," I admitted. "But I'm hot to hear about you and Terry and, I'll admit to some prurient interest in you and Dr. Daniels."

Maggie laughed. "If you have to look to your long-dead mother to feed your fantasies, dear boy, you must be getting ready to join me on the other side of the River Styx. Love to tell you about Terry. Her story's a high point in my life. David Daniels I'll leave you to reconstruct on your own. Terry's the story. David Daniels—wonderful man that he was—paved the way for Terry to claim the life she knew was hers."

It was coming back to me, a story in the Charleston *Post and Courier* a friend sent to me a few years ago.

"Was Terry that woman who scandalized Charleston when she moved back as an adult, with a family of her own, a family that didn't exactly fit the local mold?"

"That's her. Still makes me well up. She went through the long, painful, gender change at Johns Hopkins. Later, after a few brushes with near-disaster, even a brief time in jail, she became a reasonably successful fiction writer. Her own story was intriguing enough, so challenging, that she could have merely written her autobiography and passed it off as fiction. But she had too much integrity, and pride, not to mention talent, to trade on that alone."

The lights went on. "Son of a bitch, Maggie! That was Terry Robinson who did the book event at that old bookstore in Charleston the last time I came to visit you, right before you died, wasn't it? And the book she was hawking—that was the autobiography she did finally write. Right?"

"It was, Henry. I wondered if you'd put that together."

"Have I got this right? After her gender change, she married the family chauffer—black, of course—and actually conceived a child, a daughter."

"I don't wonder that you remember, Henry. Too bad you were off at school when all this was happening, because it is a great story, and it pushed every hot button in the city of Charleston. Actually made the staid old Post and Courier almost worth reading for a while.

"Every preacher in town denounced her, everyone except Andrew Vest, who compared her to Mary. That would be the Virgin Mary, not Magdalene. Though he was pretty high on the Magdalene, too."

"Did you put Terry in touch with Dr. Daniels, Maggie?"

"That detail hardly touches the courage and patience required of Terry to see it through. Yes, I did, and like to think it smoothed her way, maybe a little."

"Maggie, were you and David Daniels...lovers?" What's up with me; why do I keep doing this? This provoked laughter. Maggie's coughing, sputtering, smoker's cough used to alarm me as a kid.

"What's so funny, Maggie?"

"Well, Henry, you've always been skittish about being too much like me, nothing like your father. Not to worry; you've got plenty of your father in you. The first, sometimes the *only* thing he wanted to know if a man and woman appeared even remotely friendly—were they lovers? A man thing, going straight for the groin. Henry, despite your anxieties, for good and for ill, you *are* a man, no mistaking. It's that unexamined 'sex ahead of anything else' that makes women think no man ever really grows up. I doubt I need to remind you it nearly blew up your life more than once."

Though mercifully different now, sixty and retired, than

when I was in the thick of it, at forty, it still gave me the shivers. There'll always be a scary piece of me run by hormones, out of reason's reach.

"Were we lovers? Look, David Daniels—God love him—made it possible for Terry to claim the life she'd always known was rightfully hers. *Lover* is hardly adequate to describe what that aroused in me. Lovers? Can you come up with a better way to describe someone who arouses the most profound affection and gratitude in you, who extends himself for you, at great cost?"

"I appreciate that, Maggie, but…"

"No *but*, Henry. I stayed in touch with Terry through the nearly four years it took to complete the gender change. David was nothing short of an angel from God. And, can you imagine, when Terry and that chauffer conceived a child, I think even David regarded it as a miracle medicine couldn't have achieved."

"And what a child!"

An image flashed in my memory.

The day I went to her book signing, Terry, who must have been in her late-fifties then, was seated, hidden behind a pile of her books. I didn't see her when I first walked in. There was a young woman standing next to her—her skin the coffee color now popular in models, but then considered exotic. One of the most beautiful women I'd ever seen. Her daughter.

When I went up to speak to her—it blows my mind to realize now that's who she was!—Terry introduced me to her daughter. I was spellbound. I asked Terry to inscribe a book for Alice. Alice thought I was crazy to go to her book signing. Alice considered her story a freak show. I doubt she ever read the book. I told Terry I thought she must be the bravest person I'd ever met, going through all she did to claim her real self. Then coming back to uptight Charleston, marrying the family chauffer, having a child. I must have stood there staring at her for a long time. She was kind of hunched over the table, osteoporosis maybe, hormones? She looked up at me, big smile.

"You know what she said to me?"

"Do tell, Henry."

"She said, 'I only hope your life may turn out to be half as exciting as mine has been.' Her daughter laughed. I guess she could see how nonplussed I was. Felt like a sacred moment. What Terry said seemed like God telling Moses to leave the safety of Egypt and head out to the unknown promised land."

"I remember you telling me about that, Henry. I was so near dying then I hadn't the energy to let you know how happy I was that you met her. I might remind you that Moses never made it to the promised land." Maggie laughed.

"But he *saw* it, Maggie. Never got there, but he could see it really was over there. Kind of how I felt when I met Terry and her daughter. Moments like that give me a glimpse of what could be. I take heart, don't mind that I'll never make it all the way myself."

"You know, dear boy, one the best things in coming to the end is no longer having any choice; it's out of your hands. All shall be well, and all manner of things will be well."

Where the hell did Maggie learn about Julian of Norwich?

"Oh, my boy, the secrets that remain to be unlocked for you. You've glimpsed them, wonder whether to trust them. They're real. Including the dying everyone is scared of, that, no matter how long you keep it at bay, will have its way with you. And voila!, dying is that ecstasy we imagine but never quite find in life. Richer even than the fantasies that make old men cling to their adolescence. What a sweet moment when you told me about your meeting Terry."

"Not to mention her drop-dead, beautiful daughter."

"Yes, Henry, her too. Hang onto your boyself." Maggie laughed.

"A couple of years after you died, I saw Terry's obituary in the New York Times. It said no one in Charleston was ever sure she was for real or was a fraud."

"Of course, Henry, old Charleston. She challenged too many Charleston icons. And a lot of others. The Times hedges its bets."

"Putting these pieces together... If I hadn't been scared of where it might lead, paid more attention, to you and Terry, you and David, you and Andrew, might have spared me a lot of recriminations. Maybe way back then I could have embraced your legacy as blessing rather than burden."

"Henry, thank God you never shut yourself down, even when you felt perilously on the edge. Your nerve endings may have gone into hiding, but they didn't die. Look where we are now, you and I. What a pleasure!"

"When I came back from that visit I told Alice I knew it was the last time I would ever see you. I thought your dying would be as much relief as anguish, but it didn't let me off the hook the way I imagined. I gave Terry's book to Alice, told her about the book signing, her amazing story, her beautiful daughter. She didn't seem much interested."

"Why should she be, Henry? It's not exactly a trial lawyer's story. Freaks like us love it. But we need those tight-asses to hold things together. Our lives would be a mess if she responded to the world as we do. You're wise to mostly keep your own counsel about it. Do you hang on Alice's every word when she tells you how she saved her corporate client from the clutches of the CIA?"

My sciatic was signaling time to close this session. Maggie's right. How often Alice has come home on fire about something that happened with a client. I try to look interested but I couldn't pass a quiz on what she'd told me.

"Things come a cropper, Henry, when we let ourselves be intimidated and lose our nerve about how we see the world. Trying to stuff ourselves into their linear world only creates stress, for us, and for the linear people too.

"But we best never forget how much we need those linear types to keep us from sliding over the edge, and to make the trains run on time."

My turn to laugh. "Right, Maggie, especially when you need a good lawyer."

"Of course. And when you're looking to give some air time to the part of you that's been lurking in the shadows, look for an unmoored, dead mother."

My sciatic says "now!"

"Ready for a break, Maggie. One last thing. Would it be stretching it to say you were in love with Terry?"

54

Christ, Henry, talk about unrepentant. It's *you* that's stuck on that bronze beauty daughter. Maggie's silence was eloquent.

Maggie checked out. The air, the energy in the attic changed, like a low pressure system blowing through.

My Sisters and Me

R ELAYING BY EMAIL a purposely vague description of my encounters with Maggie, I'd persuaded my sisters to go off together for a couple of days. They're straight-shooters. Our affection and respect for each other has grown as we aged. I wasn't sure how they'd process the spook thing, but I knew they'd listen, and give me insight into what was becoming a life-changer for me.

Victoria, Jean and I hadn't spent a lot of time together since our father, our surviving parent, died fifteen years earlier. Our energies were claimed by spouses, dogs, children, mortgages, jobs, the usual emotional upheavals.

My encounters with Maggie ramped up my eagerness to see them.

Three aging flower children—the '60s our behavior lab—entertaining our share of that period's excesses, we had each emerged into middle age, and beyond, indelibly marked, grateful to be intact.

Countless hours of therapy, seven marriages among the

three of us, brushes with alcohol abuse, drugs, extracurricular sex, and random shopping, my two sisters and I put aside our distractions and scheduled what I anticipated might be our long-postponed come-to-Jesus gathering. I had teased a little about the urgency it held for me without detailing my attic conversations with Maggie.

I considered Maggie the biggest skeleton in our collective closet.

We booked rooms for two nights at an old ark of a hotel on Lake Winnipesaukee in New Hampshire. It was fall, a chill wind blew off the lake.

Three siblings, roosting in oversize wicker chairs in the hotel parlor, taking afternoon tea. By 4:30, northern New England autumn dusk turned the lake the consistency of glass. A fire, fed by massive oak logs, burned furiously in the walk-in fireplace. The room was cozy. I took a swallow of tea, gathering myself, and led off.

There was no one else in the room or I might have wimped out.

"I wonder, ladies, which parent you would say influenced you the most in how you shaped your life?"

My sisters looked at each other, then me, suspiciously.

Victoria: "If that's a serious question, Henry, how about you go first?"

"Mom," I said.

Much shifting of position in their big chairs. Faces betraying skepticism.

"Get real, Henry," Jean said, "I hope you didn't bring us all this way just to play one of those tiresome family tricks like Dad used to."

Dad? I guess it felt like a stealth attack. Jean laughed nervously.

For all of our grownup, therapy-laden years, I thought the three of us agreed. Mom's passivity, depression, alcoholism, agoraphobia caused us continuing pain. Our father received a pass. His eccentricities and weaknesses, disguised by an all-business persona, didn't arouse the same worry as how contagious our mother's phobias may have been for us.

"You mean," Victoria asked, "she was the strongest influence because you work so hard not to be like her?"

"Actually not, Victoria; not any more. I can finally say, just about every gift I use to navigate the world, I ascribe to her more than to Dad."

Pregnant pause. I supposed they were rehearsing memories of our agreement about our mother, the reclusive alcoholic. When Jean finally responded, she was pissed.

"OK, Henry," Jean's voice impatient, edgy, "what's this about? I have no interest in more Mom-slamming, but she's no role model for me."

We'd just begun and I was already exhausted.

"I know how strange this must sound. I was too chicken to ever say this out loud before. Not that I've changed my mind, but I'm ready to own up to how it was for me rather than how I thought it ought to be. I have this bad feeling that dissing Mom ended up dissing me."

Pause, Henry. Was that long enough? Christ, probably ten seconds. OK, go, Henry.

"I knew, despite her foibles, you loved her as I did, with an intensity that didn't match up with her passivity. It's primordial. She carried us in her body, constructed us out of her marrow. She was weird. So am I. What it's cost me to try to junk her. She is the source of the best parts of me. I hid that because I had no place to put it. I didn't dare, because I was afraid that meant surrendering myself to becoming lazy and unproductive, as we've always said Mom was. I was afraid that if left to my own devices, I, too, would be lazy and unproductive.

You talk too much, Henry. But, what the shit, I've got a lot to talk about. My sisters seem like they're still with me.

"Unconditional love, irrevocable connection, unmerited—I preached about it until I was sick of the sound of my own voice. I liked that it was countercultural. I didn't dare acknowledge that Maggie, boozy Maggie, was how I knew about that, not a preacher's tired cliché. It's got flesh—hers. Dysfunctional, alcoholic, agoraphobic Maggie's flesh. Who knew?"

"Jesus, Henry," Victoria said, "I think you really do get it. Maybe it's a surprise to you because you've never had a baby grow inside you and come out of your body."

Jean laughed. "Some of your parishioners called you 'Father.' But father's no more than half of it. No wonder you fretted about gender confusion. Maybe you aren't gay, but the way you made your living is packed with what's normally assigned to women."

My sisters had drained the chardonnay I had brought. I'd barely touched my beer. Good thing they'd fed that fire with a huge Yule log; we could be here a while.

"And what do you know," I said, "now I discover Alice, who could hardly stand to be in the same room with Maggie, saw all that starch in her from the start. *I* sure as hell hadn't. Or maybe I was too scared to own it. I could see Dad's side, his contempt for her weaknesses. I figured you two were pretty much the same as me."

In the silence I slipped into a reverie in front of the blazing fire. The silence and the fire felt embracing, calming.

Victoria, Jean and I, fruit of Maggie's womb. We had our innings over the years, struggling to claim our own lives. The intensity of our love for each other must be as much biology as psyche.

"I'm not sure why now, but I always wanted to tell you about two recurring dreams, nightmares. Never told you before because they reveal more than I want anyone to see. I'm getting less self-protective in my old age. Maggie's helping with that. Something about the dreams reveal a piece of me I always thought bears our dysfunctional mother's stamp."

I loved how Jean and Victoria's handsome, age-etched faces were highlighted by the crackling fire. Maybe they weren't conventionally beautiful, too old, weathered. To me they were more than beautiful, striking, Rembrandt portraits. Their lively eyes were trained on me.

"Dreams, Henry," Victoria said, "shall I break out the music so the audience doesn't miss the high drama?"

Guess I'm laying it on a little thick.

"Stick with me," I said. "The dreams are short. No sex."

"Disappointing," Jean said. Tension-breaking laugh.

"They began when I was seven or eight, visited me maybe three or four times a year until I was in my thirties. Since then only a handful of times, but still vivid."

Jean laughed. "Henry, you're a preacher-man to your bones. Lucky for us, you're more entertaining—and more screwy—than most preachers. Your dreams are probably as obscure to Victoria and me as your other visions, or for that matter, your sermons. So what? They're fun, never boring. I'd be home watching some lame Netflix if I weren't here. So go for it."

Victoria, nodding agreement, didn't crack a smile. I'd told these dreams to one colleague and a couple of shrinks, no one in the family. For years, every time I felt I'd made a breakthrough, uncovered a hidden piece of myself, these dreams would pop up, as if they'd been lurking, waiting to warn me not to risk too much.

They shifted in their chairs. Jean poured the last drops of wine into Victoria's glass, and drew in a big breath.

"Jesus, Henry," she said, "your life never lacked for drama. The cover being priest required must have taken a lot of energy."

"Acknowledged," I responded.

"In the first dream I'm crouched behind the strawberry mound in our backyard in Charleston, squinting through the sight of my rifle. I have a Japanese soldier's head in the crosshairs. My finger is frozen over the trigger. Seems an eternity. Beads of sweat break out on my forehead. As I strain to make my finger squeeze the trigger, I hear something behind me. I turn just in time to see a Japanese soldier about to run me through with his bayonet. I wake."

Wine's drained.

"Drama's too feeble a word," Victoria said.

"The other dream takes place in a well-equipped office, like Dad's office, which I only saw a couple of times. The boss comes in, asks if I've finished the report he'd asked for the day before. What report? The boss's face morphs into Dad's face. My pulse races; sweat rolls down my side. Shame, fear, nausea, I barely manage to choke back. I wake."

"Poor Henry," Victoria said, "you were more fucked up than we knew. Maybe even more than Jean and I were." The three of us dissolved into gales of laughter. "Those were pretty cool dreams; you must miss them."

My right calf suddenly seized up, rock-hard, painful charley horse. "Shit!" I leapt from my chair, my leg buckled, I staggered, nearly fell, struggled to straighten my calf.

Victoria laughed. "So Mom's haunted you all these years, has she, Henry? Well dear old Dad's doing his number on you right now, punishing you for more than not finishing that report on time. By the age you are now, he never went a night without a charley-horse."

"Goddamn it, Vic, how about a little compassion? This hurts like a bitch!" I danced around awkwardly, slowly able to reach down to massage the knot as it gradually began to release.

"Sorry, Henry, it's too ironic, the whole thing. I know you didn't identify much with Dad, thought you were a disappointment to him. Maybe because you look so much like him, have his voice, his mannerisms—sometimes you seem like his carbon copy. Even the cramps. You're not Dad, I get that, but you sure as hell aren't without a big piece of him. Sometimes when I see you from a distance, I see Dad. And you know what? My heart skips a little because I'm happy to see him. And, of course, to see you, too."

"And as for that Japanese soldier," Jean waded in, "I hope

you didn't crush any strawberries when you went down. They were better than any I've tasted since."

Big laugh, let some air out.

"Sorry, Henry," Jean said, "I know this is a big deal, but the reality is, for good and for ill, you are eerily reminiscent of him. No, not just like him, God knows. But with a big dose of the super salesman he was. You can charm a monkey out of a tree. That didn't come from Mom. She didn't give a shit about charming anyone."

I was finally able to put weight on my offending leg but didn't dare sit back down for fear of my calf seizing again.

"I've been told so often I remind people of him; sometimes that feels nice. It's not as if I *hated* him. Just that he never seemed even interested in breaking free of his Willy Loman straitjacket. I look in the mirror and see Dad, Ben, looking back at me, and, God save me, there's that stern, disapproving look that used to turn my stomach acid.

"It bugs me that I still give a shit. I know, I know, he's my father. All that therapy, to stop worrying what he thought of me. Or what I *imagined* he thought of me. Eternal damnation."

Slight twitch in the offending thigh. I danced more to keep it from taking hold. Jean and Victoria sat while I danced. The dying fire still warmed the great room.

"Maggie's helped me understand the stuff I was tuned to, most I thought best kept underground. Embracing it scared the shit out of me. Like the shelter I'd constructed for myself might collapse. How many therapists encouraged me to consider my longings legitimate? Now I know it couldn't happen until I was willing to honor in myself the weird shit I feared in Maggie. Being priest provided enough oxygen for my weird side. Maybe following Ben's lead would give me air for my more mainstream side. But I knew that would end up shutting down most of the weird side, the side that frees my passion."

Wine gone, beer warm, we'd been sitting about as long as people our age can without turning to stone or going to sleep. Losing focus.

"You know, Henry," Victoria's tone was peevish, "you may be assuming too much that Jean's and my feelings about Mom and Dad were just like yours. Yes, I got sick of her drinking, wished she hadn't closed herself off from the world, but I never felt particularly at risk that her eccentricities had crippled me.

"And, probably because I was his daughter, not his son, I never felt a lot of pressure to please Dad."

Jean nodded agreement.

"Forgive me for wanting to implicate you two in my struggles," I said, "it's just that I count on you understanding in ways no one else could. Like that demon I wrestle, accusing myself of stumbling into ordination by default, without an authentic call, scared my other choices might have been crime, or addiction, or both. Maybe a circus clown."

"You'd have made a lot more money as a second story man," Jean laughed, "and you're sillier than most clowns."

Our family's talent for diverting our dilemmas into teasing probably saved our sanity, but it also could make me feel like an asshole for taking them seriously. Well, Henry, be grateful for anything that preserves your sanity.

The oversized chairs were comfortable an hour and a

half ago, but these three old timers had reached our limit. Weariness makes us testy.

"It's not just that I feel bad, robbed, or am looking to make Maggie my scapegoat. It's this convoluted gender stuff that keeps coming up. I wondered what difference it made, being her daughters rather than her son.

"Made your choices look different from mine?"

Jean looked at her watch. "It's after six—those cramps, you're dehydrated, Henry—I'm ready for a hot bath. How about we adjourn for an hour? Meet back in your room before dinner. You got another bottle of wine in your room? A little more wine might make me willing to take a flier on what I think you're asking us."

Victoria nodded. We adjourned.

It had gotten even more chilly. Walking along the outside porch along the lake, I was weary, cold. The eerie call of a loon broke the night's stillness. The sharing with my sisters I had looked forward to was seeming more like my true confession. My leg was sore; my mind spinning. The conversations with Maggie, and now with Jean and Victoria, peeling back years and layers of illusion. Under each layer new insight. But at what cost? Sirens calling to me from the shoals?

Back to my frumpy, inn-room—double bed, uncomfortable, lumpy chair, school-room desk. I drew myself a hot bath, hotter than I'd ordinarily like. Relax that sore calf.

I fell dead asleep in the tub, woke with a sudden start not sure how long it had been. Not that long, I guess. The water was still comfortably warm, embracing. I needed that.

Out of the tub, dried, dressed in sweats, the warmest clothes I'd brought, I went down the corridor to the ice machine, came back and put a bottle of chardonnay in the ice.

I took my tattered Moleskine journal from my "man bag" (an affectation I adopted after a trip to Italy where all the cool men carry a small purse) and jotted a few thoughts:

Seminary. I didn't like thinking I chose seminary and ordination by default, just to keep my demons at bay. Ben's father was a clergyman, revered in the family. Ben may have thought preachers didn't connect with real life the way businessmen did, but his respect for—and fear of—his father, kept him from saying so out loud. He didn't accuse me of ducking real life when I told him I was going to seminary; wish I hadn't made the accusation against myself.

Ben's siblings, my uncles and aunts, all professionals—doctors, teachers, scientists. Once, testing, teasing him, I called him a capitalist pig, tarnishing our family's legacy of noble, helping professionals. "Lucky thing someone in this family goes to work every few generations to keep you dreamers alive," he'd responded. Ben never surrendered the upper hand. Certainly not to his son. Fair enough, I say now. His long, hard-working career in business was every bit as honorable as mine, or his siblings'.

But whatever drove him was pretty different from what drove Maggie. But then, she wasn't afraid of God. I suspect Ben was. What the hell, she didn't believe in God. For Ben, God was like oxygen: just because you don't really know anything about it, you don't stop breathing. Neither Maggie nor I could never settle, let it be.

My sisters, my flesh and blood, showed up early. As I shifted the two chairs to face the bed, came a knock. Before I could answer, they entered the unlocked door.

Jean looked elegant in red blouse, long skirt, and deep green cashmere sweater. Great look. "Love your shoes, I said, "they match your outfit."

"How do you like *my* outfit?" Victoria asked, twirling theatrically in the small space between the bed and the window. "Perfect," I answered, glad I wasn't the only one in sweats. Victoria, two years older than I, and Jean a little more than two years younger, handsome, well-preserved women. They'd absorbed their share of knocks, weathered them pretty nicely. Proud to call them my sisters. I knew I could count on them being straight with me, but never cruel.

A Reckoning

W E SETTLED IN, I handed them each a cracker with a slice of Port Salut cheese—classy choice, Henry.

Victoria jumped right in: "Henry it would help Jean and me if you'd fill us in on what you're looking for from us, maybe a little more about what's changing thanks to whatever these Maggie moments are for you. If it's late-life therapy, we're all for it, but we may not be the best ones to see you through it."

I smiled as I poured them each a glass of chardonnay. Leaning back on the king size bed, looking at my sisters seated in those vintage, Holiday Inn, uncomfortable chairs, I was touched by how much they meant to me. Not only savvy, no bullshit women, but always willing to hang in with me, even when I was hovering on the edge of self-destruction. I had pulled the curtain across the window, the 40 watt table lamp provided dim light. Kind of wonderful, we three who had shared so much, knee-to-knee in a hotel room all these years later.

"Fair question, Vic; I've been asking myself the same thing. No doubt there's the therapy dimension, but there's something more pressing, for me. And maybe for you two.

"Everyone born in the 1940s, like us, has lived through a time that has been thoroughly catalogued. But I don't think anyone yet has a good handle on just what our legacy is. The prevailing ethic in our house—don't rock the boat—was pretty ordinary, I think, for middle class families of the time. Yet each of us have spent significant pieces of our lives rocking lots of boats.

"I'm finding out that our passive mother wasn't all that passive. But she was hidden, clever. I was much less so. Which is why I missed most of her nuance."

I interpreted their wide smiles as: "Oh bravo for you, Henry; you're waking up."

"Victoria, you were a feminist before there was a name for it, and Jean, you fought for early childhood education when Head Start was way in the future. Would it be offbase to say that letting your convictions lead, cost you at least one husband each?

"And, Victoria, once feminism lodged in your bones, seemed like you opted out on marriage altogether."

"I didn't come here to talk about all that, Henry," Victoria said. "I grant you, my two marriages didn't make me eager to try a third, but hardly because I was brave. Just weary of tying myself in knots to try to keep a husband from feeling unappreciated. I know you're looking to make your anti-war stuff, civil rights protests, women's ordination that made waves in your churches, all legitimate spending of your energy. Not to mention your passion for writing poetry. Maybe

Jean and I are strong-willed; maybe we appear brave to you. But you had an issue we didn't—having to keep a congregation of nervous people happy while we did our thing."

"I didn't show my poetry to parishioners; maybe slipped in a few lines in sermons, always cautiously obscure. I get more credit than I deserve for my part in the civil rights and anti-war stuff. I wasn't in the vanguard of women's ordination. I was cautious, a follower, not a leader."

"Oh, that old-boy modesty—a legacy from dear old Dad. So you were tentative, cautious. Big deal. So is everyone at the start of a movement, if they don't have a death wish. Events push them deeper, the way they did you. You hung in. Besides, I like bragging on my little brother."

"Nice, Victoria. I didn't mean to ask for that. I was hoping you'd help me get a handle on how where we came from makes sense of who we've turned out to be. I'm learning some stuff I never knew about our family, both sides, that makes looking in the mirror different."

"How about a refill on that, Henry?" Jean asked, holding her glass while I poured.

"No sociologist looking at our family would have predicted how we three have spent our lives. Ben was a '50s company man if there ever was one, a corporate soldier. Maggie was, by every outward measure, eminently forgettable, except maybe for her pathologies, agoraphobic, alcoholic."

Jean interrupted impatiently. "So? So we're misfits. What's new? Portraying ourselves that way was a backhand way of congratulating ourselves for not being like everyone else. God forbid. How unseemly, how un-Simpson like to be ordinary. Do we really need to plow that old ground again?"

I took my first slug of wine, fluffed up the pillow, re-arranging my position, spare my sciatic, stalling for time, mulling over a response.

"I suspect there's a piece of us that's always homeless, ev-erywhere," I said. "A genetic piece we can trace. A loneliness at our core. I wonder, do you feel like unsettled outsiders, everywhere? I do. Tried sex, drugs, alcohol, tennis, poetry, meditation—even considered religion—looking to make peace with that feeling of being outlier?"

"Cool, Henry," Victoria said. "I love feeling exotic. You describe a lot of what my life is like. But don't you think you're straining at gnats to make us Simpsons more exotic than we really are?"

I laughed. "No doubt, Victoria. But not totally. Maggie's determination not to let the culture define her for sure created her isolation, but it had integrity I didn't get at the time."

The chardonnay was running low, my sisters can hold it.

"Must be a bigger issue for you," Jean said. Victoria nod-ded. "Her integrity isn't a surprise to me. How come it is for you?"

"What the fuck, Jean, I *am* Maggie, in male drag. Luckily my choices about how to be contrary haven't resulted in my becoming a reclusive alcoholic. Damn near did. I wasn't into the gay thing, but I sure as hell never fit comfortably into most of male culture. I wondered if I was one of those guys closeted not only from the world, but from myself. Scared the shit out of me.

"I kept wanting to connect with women, thought the

right woman could sanction me. confirm my maleness. Nearly sealed my doom, as you may remember."

"Jesus, Henry," Jean said, "you lucked out, marrying Alice. I hate to think how things might have turned out otherwise. I worried that Alice would get fed up with those women fawning over you, might tell you to take a hike. Alice may not be easy to get close to, but she's real, one tough, smart lady. Got her act together. She saved your ass more ways than you'll ever know."

I excused myself to go for a pee. Splashed water on my face, a couple of deep breaths, things getting a little close. I was remembering that conversation with Maggie when I told her Alice and I were getting married.

"No question" I said when I returned, "Alice has been my anchor to windward, kept me from capsizing more than once".

"And you hers, I might add," Jean said. "Quite wonderful how you plug the gaps in each other's world."

"A geneticist," I said, "might say resistance to letting the culture smother our passion, comes from the XX chromosome in our family more than the XY."

I sipped my wine.

"How exactly do you get that, Henry?" Jean asked, her face arranged skeptically.

"I've spent my life running from everything Maggie in me. I have the normal guy thing about being a fully realized man, and it made me uneasy that what has mattered most to me came from my mother, whom I considered barely functional."

They both laughed. "Nobody who has followed your kick-ass career in the church would guess that you were shaped by your passive, alcoholic, agoraphobic mother," Jean said.

"Nor," Victoria added, "would those women you had near career-ending closecalls with wonder whether you were an authentic guy."

This was fun, if a little scary. Only my sisters could weave such rich fabric from what seemed to me meager threads. It was late; we were getting close to the bone.

"We need to go to dinner before the dining room closes," I said. "There's some mind-boggling stuff I learned about Maggie's mother, our Nana, that lights up this contrary gene. Even meshes with a similar gene I'd never have guessed in company-man Ben's family."

The hostess seemed none too happy to see us coming into the dining room only a half hour before closing. I tried to ignore her glare. Neither Jean nor Victoria seemed to notice it. It's her job, Henry, you're a paying customer.

We didn't order drinks; we'd had our share. The only other people in the dining room left before our dinner arrived. We tucked into the warm bread. While we waited I began telling them what I'd learned about Maggie's family in Cuba.

Havana, Cuba
1902

A NOTHER DAY MAGGIE'S BOOK fell open to the Ds, de Murias, Maggie's maiden name. The D page in that little book was packed.

"I bet you remember that photograph, people on a balcony in Havana. The man is Ramon Andres Ignacio de Murias y Sentmanat, our great grandfather. The little girl is Sylvia Angela, eight years old, Maggie's mother, our grandmother. That's the balcony of the Hotel Inglaterra. It's May 20, 1902, Cuban Independence Day. The first President, Tomas Estrada Palma, had been sworn in that afternoon. With them are friends, the de la Guardia family.

"We all know the photo, but I'd never been sure where it was taken, or what the occasion was.

"How you do know all that, Henry?" Victoria asked. "Love seeing Nana as a little girl. Love her fierce expression."

"What can I tell you? From Maggie. Maybe I had an epileptic vision. I saw our great-grandparents and grandmother watching the inaugural parade of the first President of the Republic of Cuba. From a pretty sweet spot, wouldn't you say?"

"Mom told you all that? That's some hell of a séance you're having up in your attic," Jean said. "Don't take anti-seizure medicine until you're through with this."

"Stirring," I agreed. "Don't you love that we have this photo of our great-grandparents and grandmother on that historic occasion? I figured they must have been a big deal. Cuba, finally freed from Spain. They had to have been well connected to be up on the balcony of that ornate building, not down on the street with the hoi polloi."

My sisters seemed mesmerized, as I had been when Maggie told me all this. I was grateful they didn't push me any harder about how I knew this.

"I'm just glad we didn't throw this out when we cleaned out Maggie's apartment," I said.

"The photo is misleading. Yes, our ancestors on that balcony are wealthy, well-placed. But the truth about them, and about Cuba, flies in the face of our history books about what was happening in Cuba when that photo was taken.

"Our Uncle Ramon and Maggie wouldn't be born for more than a decade, but the seeds of their character, and ours, were there, germinating genetic code—Ramon's, Maggie's, yours and mine. Waiting to be assembled."

I shifted position, sciatic, give them a chance to consider.

Victoria smiled. "I always wished I lived close enough to come to your church, Henry. Not a lot of fretting about needing to believe in God. Whatever reason people came, your preaching, a cross between Grimm's fairy tales and the

Zen of Alan Watts, must have been great fun. Maybe even reassuring for the adventuresome few."

"Thanks, Vic, I'd like to think so. The credit, if credit is what's deserved, belongs to our mother. I'd have read into the picture the opposite of the truth."

"The de Muriases were important people in Havana, but they weren't boosters of the newly inaugurated Estrada Palma. They were clandestinely supporting the handful of intellectuals, and larger group of peasants, already plotting to overthrow him. Of course Palma and his henchmen were unaware of that at the time this picture was taken."

"Give me a break," Jean said, "Nana's family were revolutionaries? She was one cool woman, but..."

"I know, Jean. She died when I was six, so can't say I remember her that well. Turns out Maggie was cut from her cloth. The opposite of what she appeared. Nana's parents, Nana herself, were pretty radical activists.

"The American General, Leonard Wood, was military governor of Cuba until Palma was elected, in a rigged election. Palma lived in New York City. He hadn't set foot on the island for decades. He was an American citizen, for God's sake. Does that sound like the election of a Cuban nationalist? The de Murias family didn't think so. And General Wood was there that day to give him the American imprimatur."

"Wait a minute, Henry," Victoria interrupted, "General Wood? Not the same General Wood: that white-haired, bent-over old man we used to see at the Manila Polo Club when we were teenagers? Wasn't he Governor General of the Philippines after WWII, before Quirino was elected?"

"Same guy, Victoria. Blew my mind, too. Had to have been nearly 100 by then. That we knew him made me feel at least a little connected to Nana and Cuba. Nana's parents had no more use for General Wood than Maggie did a generation later when we were living in Manila.

"When I told Maggie I remember people at the Polo Club treating General Wood like a tin god, Maggie laughed. She said that was a source of friction between her and Ben. She thought the old guy was a stuffed shirt, a repulsive colonialist. Guess that really pissed Ben off."

"He's a bit player in our story. Ben bought him drinks, toadied up to him. Maggie held him in contempt. He had been part of what her grandparents opposed in Cuba.

"Maybe it seems a big jump, from Nana's family opposing Estrada, to our decision to demonstrate against the Viet Nam War, march for civil rights, women's rights, but seems to me we were cooked in the same pot."

My dinner was cold. The chicken looked tired. I'd sated myself on cheese and wine back in the room. My sisters reminisced about dinners at the Polo Club, tottering, old General Wood receiving obeisance from expat sycophants, including Ben, while Maggie muttered unkind words under her breath. Victoria and Jean loved remembering that. The waitress cleared their plates. I hoped my sisters weren't sick of this yet.

"You feeling patient?" I asked, apologetic for hogging the conversation.

"Patient enough, Henry," Jean said, "only because you're a natural born raconteur. But you haven't touched your supper."

"I'm not really hungry, at least not as hungry for this sad looking chicken as I am to catch you two up on my conversations with Maggie."

"Fire away," Victoria said. I pushed the uninviting plate to one side and went on channeling Maggie.

⌒

I had expressed surprise about the role of Maggie's family.

"'Right, Henry,' Maggie said, 'it's never simple, figuring out who's on which side.'

"I told her it seemed maybe arrogant, or dishonest, certainly disloyal, enjoying the perks of being in the favor of a regime you're working to topple."

"Maggie agreed it takes arrogance. Seems simpler, sometimes sensible, to go along. Maybe, God-forbid, we consider allegiance to conscience a higher good than loyalty. 'It damn-straight better make us nervous to assume our conscience is more finely tuned than those on the other side.' Maggie teased me: 'How about your chronic quarrel with the Church, Henry? Talk about disloyal.'"

Jean jumped in. "So in these conversations with Maggie you were up to your old tricks: looking to rationalize the double agent you were as a parish priest. God's man pushing against the church. Oh man, Henry, do you ever get yourself mixed up with Jesus, turning over the moneychangers' tables in the temple? Only difference between you and Jesus is they didn't give Jesus a membership in the country club.

Ooh, right to the quick, Jean.

"I'll never work out how much I hid my ambivalence behind my feigned innocence."

"I never bought it, Henry," Jean said.

"Well, without meaning to exonerate myself, I can honestly say I was at least partially unaware of that. I'm more sorry now for my lack of awareness than I am for my duplicity.

"You'll like what Maggie said: 'That's why your sisters tease you about looking so much like Ben. You *look* the part. OK, maybe you don't fit the whole package. You were never too proud to cozy up to the power brokers when you needed them to have your back. And you didn't do much to disturb the façade. You and Andrew Vest—bow ties, great backhand, martinis—clinched your place in their clubs. Never a comfortable fit, was it? You were designed to be a counter spy, a curse imbedded in your ancestry.'"

"Oh, the drama!" Victoria said.

"Maggie laughed about that, too, though I can't say I immediately appreciated the humor. That narrow line between appearance and the reality it so often hid required doing a hell of an intricate dance. Left me constantly looking for someplace I could relax and dare to be myself. Someplace I could call home."

"*Home?*" Victoria interjected. "You expected to find somewhere you would actually feel at home?"

"No, actually. Though I never lost my wistfulness about that, I knew it was not to be. My first year in seminary my Hebrew scripture professor explained that Hebrew—*habiru*—means wanderer, a wandering nobody, no clear identity. I felt like he was talking about me."

"Where does Alice come down on all this?" Jean wondered. "She's one tough cookie, nobody's liege woman, but she spends her days imbedded with the suits."

"I never get into this much with Alice. She thinks it's pointless self-diddling. Alice does tasks, not identity. You want to fight the establishment; go for it. You want to throw in your lot with trouble makers, fine; do it. But spare her the emotional drama."

"God, Henry, how did you ever luck into marrying her?"

"Usual way, ladies; not luck. You'll never know what a tiger I am between the sheets."

"Spare us, Henry," Victoria laughed.

"Maggie said more that day, if you've got the patience, and they don't kick us out of the dining room. How about we order a cappuccino to stall them?"

We did. I continued.

"Maggie was finely tuned to why all this mattered to me so much.

"'Those are our kin on that balcony,'" she said, 'in more than just genes. The people on the street below, rabble, jammed shoulder to shoulder, watching the parade, saw them the way many of your parishioners saw you. Respected, feared, a little envied, resented. You, living in those grand, church-owned houses. Most assumed the de Muriases were carrying water for Estrada Palma and his American handlers, the way your parishioners assumed you were guardian of the ecclesiastical status quo.'"

"Oh, man," Jean said, "she laid it on you pretty thick, didn't she?"

"It gets richer," I said.

"Estrada Palma assumed our great grandfather was on board. He offered him the Finance portfolio in his cabinet. Nothing about him had betrayed his true leanings. He was *of* them, but he was not *with* them. Traitor to his class, what Ben used to accuse FDR of. You understand, don't you, Henry?'"

"Then—sorry ladies, there's no way to soften this; I actually overheard the conversation between our great-grandparents on that balcony. Call it a dream if you like."

"Henry, you're the ringmaster; carry on," Jean said. Had there been a congregation as willing as my sisters to suspend disbelief, I might still be preaching.

"'Surely you feel hypocritical, Ramon,' our great grandmother said, her voice laced with sarcasm, 'standing up here as if we believed we were celebrating Cuba's freedom, the way all those people down there believe. We know the ugly reality. Estrada is president only because he and the United States have an understanding he will do their bidding?'"

"I'm here to tell you," I said to my sisters, "*that* would have intimidated me: her withering stare, challenging voice. If Great Grandfather Ramon found it unsettling, he didn't betray it, either in manner or voice."

"He was one slick dude. 'My darling Angel,' he said unctuously, 'reality seldom conforms to our ideals. Our lifelong mutual hatred of injustice forms a central piece of our love for each other. I daresay there's hardly been a single moment for either of us in which the affluence and privilege into which we were born failed to discomfort us. The new president may be no greater hypocrite than you or I, were we to measure our egalitarian beliefs against the reality of our circumstances.'"

"Wow, touché!" Jean said, seeming not the least put off by the weirdness of my channeling our ancestors. "You go, Ramon!"

"Our great-grandmother's nose wrinkled, as if she'd smelled something unpleasant."

"'I'll thank you not to use your diplomatic twaddle with me, Ramon. Our prosperity may cause us discomfort, but we remain steadfast in the struggle, however hidden it must be, for true independence of our tiny country. And justice for our fellow, mostly impoverished, Cubans. This is a cruel, hypocritical moment, celebrating as if we had succeeded. Those cheering people lining the streets are facing even crueler servitude than before. We know the truth, Ramon, of our sham enthusiasm for sham independence. Our Spanish masters may have been arbitrary, but at least we were under no illusion. The United States has clandestinely replaced Spain as our master. It will come to grief.'"

"Our great-grandfather smiled—no, smirked. He'd infuriated Sylvia. Like Ben's supercilious smile when he meant to diminish Maggie. Talk about generation to generation."

"So our great-grandfather married a woman like Alice," Jean interjected, "Alice never rolls over and plays dead for you the way Maggie often seemed to for Ben. I daresay it's never a mystery to you what Alice thinks."

"Oh, so right," I admitted.

"Did you ever worry," Victoria asked, "that part of what you inherited was that ability to appear one way while actually believing something quite opposite? Maybe the skill to preach persuasively when you weren't much persuaded, or even sure you believed in God?"

On that note, we adjourned. Victoria hadn't seemed to fire that barb with quite the power I felt when it penetrated.

If there was any coming out of the closet for me, owning up to the conflict she'd asked about, was it.

⌒

I slept hard that night, dreamt both nightmares, but they ended differently. In the war dream I put down my rifle, picked a ripe strawberry and ate it. So sweet. The Japanese soldier evaporated.

In the other dream I didn't recognize the boss, who went out of his way to thank me for going the extra mile with that report that wasn't due for another week.

I arrived in the dining room to find my sisters already well into their breakfast. The day had turned cold and sunny, the kind that gives me energy. Forced paper-whites decorated each table, giving a sweet scent to the sun-filled room. My sisters' warm greeting made me feel they, too, were in good form.

"Good morning, dear sisters, what's for breakfast?"

"The omelet is very tasty," Victoria said, "stuffed with really sharp cheddar."

"Sounds great!"

"Good," she said, "because we already ordered one for you."

Curb your petulance, Henry, it's affection, not control. "Thank you, ladies, nice to know you were thinking of me,"

I lied. I sat at the place they'd left between them, penned between two strong women. But happy, right Henry, to be connected to such fine, sturdy women? And to think they love you.

I told them about my nightmares having happy endings.

"Well done," Jean said, "Victoria and I can claim royalties for remixing your dreams? Next thing you'll tell us you're so at home with yourself, you actually *do* believe in the Trinity after all. That's where you'll leave me in your dust."

Jean laughed. "I never cared whether you believed in the Trinity. Your transparent humanity, especially the way you supported women whose husbands treated them like airheads, was more proof of your piety than any creed."

"You know," I said, not sure I was up for another run of this before we parted, "once I got it that the creed and Bible were legend, metaphor, the whole business kind of lost its hold on me until I ran into the guy who had the idea Jesus was about resisting domination, in any form. That rang my bell."

"It took me three tries," Jean said, "to find a husband who didn't measure success by how dominant he is. Women in our line have been models for rewriting that code: strong, loving, enabling, not subservient. Love it that you're seeing that in our mother. We didn't come from a vacuum."

The omelet and the conversation were both delicious.

"I'm hardly the only guy I know flummoxed by the gender thing. Guess a lot of women, sponsoring equality, against domination, have been more savvy about this."

"You know, Henry," Victoria said, "we grew up just as that dominant male thing was having its last hurrah, desperately trying to preserve itself. After WWII, people moving into cities, the G.I. bill offering a new group a shot at middle class, all the old rules about to change.

"Ben felt badly about not having gone to war. He didn't think tropical disease was legitimate absolution. He wanted to make you the warrior he was ashamed of not having been."

He did? The omelet all of a sudden lost my interest. What was that moment when Ben was leaving on a trip, turned to me: "You're the papa, now."

"You were strung together more like Mom, Maggie, than like Ben." Victoria continued, interrupting my daydream. "Your strengths are understated, not the kind men curry. Ordination was a godsend—pun intended. Made your strengths pluses, not liabilities, but I knew you never considered yourself quite legitimate."

"Well, thanks, Victoria, you could have saved me a shit-load of shrink bills if we'd had this conversation a few decades ago."

Jean laughed. "Like good wine, Henry, in it's time. Don't forget all the times we bitched to each other about Mom letting Dad have the last word, when she knew he was wrong. We cheered for you to resist imitating him."

"You did? I don't remember that."

Same family, same vintage, radically different memories of how power flowed between genders in our family.

"I looked forward to this," I said, "but it's been different, really better than I hoped. I so appreciate you two making the effort."

"You want to know something, Henry," Jean said. "Way back when you told us you were getting ordained, and then you were going to marry Alice, I figured we'd lost you, the only brother we'd ever have. Neither of the stereotypes those raised for me fit the you I prized as my brother.

"You think there was a lot you didn't see in Mom or our grandparents; well, there was a ton I didn't see in you. I should have known you could never become the pious wimp I worried ordination, and marrying such a strong woman, might turn you into. I couldn't have pictured how you'd fashion both ordination and marriage to fit the Henry I loved growing up. Not only still my wonderful brother, but my wonderful brother all grown up, full of piss and vinegar. Who'd have thunk it?"

Victoria dabbed her eyes with her napkin. I studied my feet.

"Yeah," I said, "my friends worried that I'd become a pious, a doormat. Closest to a playboy among my friends, came to the church where I was doing field work my third year in seminary. Heard me preach. "'Jesus Christ, Henry,'" he said, "'scrunched up in that back pew, I thought, 'What the fuck? If this can happen to him, it can happen to anyone.'"

"I became cautious around you two, mostly avoided you. I was uncomfortable in my own skin. Thought I needed to become someone I knew I wasn't. What to make of myself, a priest who doubted religion's God, and a husband who wasn't in charge in his own house.

"Before Maggie showed up in our attic, I figured I'd go to my grave feeling that way about myself, the way I thought she had. Now I know it wasn't true about her, and I'm closer now than I ever imagined to claiming myself: wobbly priest, introvert, free lance poet, house-husband."

We embraced, said our goodbyes, finessed our old habit of hollow promises about getting together again soon.

Lovely drive home, through storybook New Hampshire small towns, time to reflect. Maggie'd promised more if I wanted to keep going. Everything felt unpredictable. If I keep going with this, how might it change how just-the-facts Alice and I had worked things out?

Blinding sunshine reflected off the snow, a day New Englanders pity friends who flee to the sunbelt for winter. Many oaks still had their brown leaves, bending under the snow, a perfect winter palette.

I arrived home around 4pm, the sun was already low, clouds begun to gather. The deep reds in the western sky, New England winter sunset, a kaleidoscope.

Walking into the house from the garage, the only light in the house came from Alice's study. She had a fire blazing in the Rumford fireplace. On her desk her MacBook, a yellow pad and pencil. The card table next to the desk, strewn with various shaped scraps of paper. Familiar scene when she's preparing an opening or closing argument. She worked harder on these than I ever had on sermons. Maybe not harder than my composing poetry.

She looked up as I entered the room. "How was your visit with your sisters?"

"Great," I answered, stifling my impulse to go into detail. Frustrating for a preacher. I tried to remember how much I resent it when Alice tries to start conversation when I'm concentrating. Tried to curb feeling hurt that she didn't stop to engage me.

"I'm pretty busy," she said, "likely will be, long into the night. Sorry not to have given much thought to supper. I figured Sunday night, finger-supper. There are a couple of hard boiled eggs, some bread, hummus in the fridge. I picked up a pint of that Ben & Jerry's pistachio you like."

You see, Henry, she *does* care, does look after you.

"Sounds good. I've been stuffing myself this weekend. How about I fix us each a plate?"

"Oh, thanks, Henry, I really need to keep going on this. You go ahead. Not sure when I'll get to food, let alone bed. Hope you don't feel abandoned."

Alice knew I would. But I've learned not to act petulant. She knew I recover quickly enough.

"Abandoned? By you, Alice? God forbid."

"Seems God did forbid my abandoning you, Henry, which explains why, despite endless attempts by nearly irresistible men to seduce me, I'm still here after all these years."

No wonder her acquittal rate exceeded that of even the firm's storied, senior lawyers.

I'm happy God forbade Alice to abandon me, and assigned me a life surrounded by strong women (assigned, Henry, not condemned). Good thing, since such a big piece of parish ministry was spending working days among women. Having two sisters and no brother wasn't bad preparation, but it fell short of teaching me how to read women's minds.

"Well, glad to be home, Alice, I missed you. Gabby been fed and walked?"

"Do I look like I've had time for that, Henry?"

On our walk I mulled over how my sisters provided simpatico company, but still, in odd ways, left me feeling alone. Maggie-time was like emotional acupuncture: sharp, healing jabs in chronically tender places. The pain quite bearable, and grateful that, even at my age, long-stuck parts of me can get moving. Interesting that Victoria and Jean weren't stuck in the same places I was.

Distracted, content to be patient with Gabby sniffing every shrub. Clear, cold night.

"Hey, Henry, what's going on?"

I hadn't seen Andrea, the youngish (fifty is youngish now, Henry?) divorcee walking her toy dachshund. The house she'd moved into at the end of the street was on the market for almost a year. There had been rumors of foreclosure before Andrea appeared. I was happy it sold, worried what sort of person might end up buying it in the bank's short sale. Some revolutionary you are Henry, worrying about your house's value. Andrea added a welcome dimension to my fantasies. Not stunningly beautiful, but something comforting, inviting about her small, compact frame, her cheerful, welcoming smile. I'd learned from near disasters as a priest that a woman's friendly façade was better met with prudence than with unchecked enthusiasm.

"Andrea! How nice to see you."

Half-true. It's nice to meet an attractive woman, but tonight I was preoccupied with Maggie, and with my sisters. And, hate to admit, maybe a little bruised by Alice's unenthusiastic welcome home.

"I hadn't expected to run into you walking your dog in

the evening. I thought you worked the graveyard shift at the hospital." Careful, Henry, don't give her the impression you're keeping track of her.

"They're jigging around with our hours at the hospital, trying to keep from having to lay off people; I only work until five on Fridays."

"Oh dear." Dispassionate concern is OK, Henry, just don't crank up one of your pastoral rescue missions. "I trust *your* job is secure." (And you can pay your mortgage.)

"Thanks for your concern, Henry. I'm pretty senior; I don't think my job's in jeopardy. But in this economy you don't dare assume it can't happen to you."

Enough, Henry, time to back off. "No, of course not. But I'm glad to know you're in a strong position. Love to chat, Andrea, but I'm the designated cook tonight." Well done, Henry; dutiful husband. Gabby and Andrea's sawed-off dachshund were taking turns sticking their noses in each other's rear ends.

"Be well, Henry." Andrea smiled sunnily as she turned around.

"And you, Andrea." I gave Gabby's leash a yank and we moved down the street. Ever since I hit puberty I required a moment to gather myself after even the most casual encounter with an attractive woman. All that stuff about being designed to reproduce your DNA captures a hell of a lot of your energy. Worlds better at sixty than at forty, but unlike bodies, fantasies don't always conform to the biological calendar.

Gabby put on the brakes, pulling against the leash,

straining to get under some low bushes. A whiff of skunk, I dragged him away. Out of range of the offending scent, I was happy to let him sniff, while I allowed myself a flashback of a life among so many women.

I am both grateful and sorry that I was more spectator than participant in the sixties sexual revolution. I did follow with great interest the awakening scholarly interest in sexuality among some early Christian communities. Passion, we finally admitted, referred not only to Jesus's suffering.

Truth is, those who explored changing sexual mores weren't sure when it was just plain coupling or when it was something more otherworldly. Alice insisted we weren't picky which.

Many hours of therapy, plus a couple of heart-stopping near scandals, convinced me that, whatever historians made of early Christians' intimate life, and however seriously the old mores were being challenged, trying to translate all that into middle class American parish life was a train wreck looking to happen.

Henry, all this for a two minute encounter with Andrea?

Still preoccupied when "Henry!" startled me again. I hadn't seen Alexander, the other man in the neighborhood who didn't go off to an office each morning. We ran into each other on our dog walks more often than I would have chosen.

Unlike me—retired early thanks to the Church Pension Fund—Alexander was a trust-fund baby. Never had a day job. Ease up on the contempt, Henry, you're an easy target yourself. Alexander considered himself expert in nearly everything, the kind of over-educated bore I'd hoped retiring might spare me. OK, Henry, maybe just a little contempt won't kill you.

"No doubt you've been following events in the Middle East!" Alexander said, his expression know-it-all smug.

Not so much as a "Good Evening." And so fucking eager, as if he was talking about the Super Bowl. I bet he doesn't even know who played in the Super Bowl.

"I suppose everyone has, Alexander." Might I call you Alex; why must it be Alexander? Easy, Hank. Henry. OK, plaguing inner voice, cut me some slack. The guy's an insufferable asshole.

"Incredible, isn't it, Henry? Which of us could have imagined Mubarak and his sons peacefully surrendering power? Why, only a couple of days ago they were vowing they would never leave."

I know your game, Alexander. You could give a shit about Egypt; you just want to be sure I know you've got the inside skinny from those thugs at Goldman who hang out with cabinet members and ramp up your fortune with default swaps. Civil, Henry, before your envy leads you someplace you don't want to go. I struggled to keep my tone scorn-free.

"I suppose there's no one so powerful they don't have a drop-dead point."

Alexander's furrowed brow signaled his disgust with my response. It was pretty lame, Henry.

"I'm afraid it's a good deal more complex than that, as you no doubt understand, Henry. The Sunnis and Shiites are squaring off in the showdown that's festered in that region for generations. Had not western colonialism, the Brits, the

French, now us, kept those thugs from cutting each other's throats, this would have blown up a lot sooner. Egypt is just the tip of the Middle East iceberg."

"I wouldn't imagine icebergs last long in the desert, do they Alexander?" No sooner out of my mouth than I wished I'd disciplined my sarcasm.

"Perhaps you've yet to grasp the gravity of this for us in this country as well, Henry." Alexander's face puckered, as if he'd tasted a sour lemon. "We still depend on that region for more than a third of our energy needs."

I knew I was going to regret my petulance trumping my judgment: "So *that's* why it cost me over fifty bucks to fill my truck yesterday."

"Nice running into you, Henry. You could do yourself a favor and take a look at The Economist's coverage this week. No one is exempt from the consequences of this one. It behooves us all to stay informed."

Behooves? I'll give you this, Alexander; you're slicker at dismissing someone when they won't play your one-up game than I ever was. My life would have been less cluttered had I learned to get rid of bores like you as efficiently. "Be kind to yourself, Alexander."

I would once have obsessed over that aborted exchange, imagining how Alexander was going to describe it to Muffy. Christ, Henry, *Muffy*? You actually give a shit what *Muffy* thinks of you? Oh yeah, in fact the embarrassing truth is you do. She's an airhead, but such a cute airhead. Worth a few late-life fantasies. As Alexander walked away, Gabby continued marking every bush and tree. Could he possibly have any more pee in those kidneys? Maybe he just leaves a whiff, an alert for other dogs that he's still around. Sort of the way you do, Henry, with your sharp tongue.

Mr. Hait's fourth-form English class, I was being a smartass: "Henry," he shouted, "you have a dog's philosophy; if you can't eat it or screw it, you piss on it." Guffaws from the others in the class. I was secretly pleased. Forty-five years later, something in me still enjoys being beyond redemption. Maybe why every sermon you ever preached had the identical refrain: "The only thing we can count on is God's indelible love." If God could love Henry Simpson, God could love anyone. Give it a rest, Henry. When did you last spend a serious moment worrying about whether God loves you? You'd happily settle for Alice, or *Maggie* loving you. Maybe even Andrea. Or Muffy? Gabby?

I arrived home, let Gabby off the leash, looking forward to a cup of tea before bed. I opened the door from the garage into the kitchen to the smell of sautéing onions. Lights on in the kitchen, Alice at the stove, wearing an apron.

"What's up, Alice? I didn't expect to see you again tonight."

"Hey Babe, you've had an adventure, I thought an omelet might taste good."

"Sweet, Alice. But what about all that stuff you're working on?"

"It'll keep, Henry. What won't is a chance for some quiet time together. I get so focused on beating up those other lawyers, sometimes I forget to enjoy my nice life having hooked up with you."

Easy does it, Henry. Too much kindness makes you suspicious; give it a chance. "Oh, Alice, thank you. Sometimes I feel like such a drone. Except for feeding and walking Gabby, occasionally providing you with decidedly non-gourmet dinners, I don't do much to justify my existence around here."

"Well, dear guy, that's just not so. You're the most generous-spirited person I know. If it weren't for your tempering influence, I'd long ago have become the monster all those guys at the firm already think I am."

I laughed. "Being a wimp has its uses, I guess." Fishing, Henry?

"Henry, wimp you're not. Your sisters are right. You may not subscribe to everything in the creed, but you live as if the Jesus love-stuff most people think is utopian, or maybe just plain bullshit, might actually be worth a try."

I didn't remember Alice ever saying anything quite like this before; it took me by surprise. I had to stop myself from protesting how far I felt from the person she described.

"Jesus, Alice, I've already left you everything in my will; what more are you schlepping for?"

Alice laughed. "How about cutting us a couple of pieces of that sourdough bread and putting them in the toaster, before this conversation gets even sloppier? I love you, Henry. I know I don't always act like it."

"Without objection," I replied, feeling pleasure begin to stir in my heart and even in my aging groin. Could it be that Alice senses the fantasies I entertained on the walk?

"For whatever reason," she said, "that dingbat who's been such a pain finally gave up stiff-arming me during today's deposition. Having him yield to me gave me good energy, so I stopped by Whole Foods on my way home and picked up a few organic vegetables. If you wouldn't mind finishing sautéing them, we can serve them with the omelet."

"Like nothing better," thrilled at the evening's unexpected turn. "Why don't you draw yourself a hot bath and I'll finish up here."

During dinner Maggie rattled on about how intense the case was becoming. Torn between the sensible wish to settle, and eagerness to test herself in courtroom combat, she rehearsed her case over dinner. Preoccupied with my attic encounters with Maggie, I had a hard time staying with the complexities. Alice was rehearsing her arguments; she wasn't looking for a response.

Delicious dinner. I finished the dishes and walked out to the living room, looking forward to getting into the New Yorker that arrived in the afternoon mail. Alice would be back in her study polishing her brief.

As I went through the living room door she intercepted me, embraced me. What's this?

"What do you say, Hen, we don't read ourselves to sleep tonight?"

Embarrassing, the pleasure, and fright, she aroused in me. So seldom lately, I figured that chapter was about closed. Not thrilled about that, but it did take some of the pressure off; will-we-or-won't-we? Whose turn is it to get it started?

"Oh, Allee, what a happy invitation!"

I meant it, even if I wondered—hoped—I was up to it. Stoked, as I felt the old juices began to stir.

Alice was usually the initiator, and she was tonight. But she'd left her aggressive-lawyer person at the office. Gentle, seductive. I responded eagerly, almost as if it were an elicit affair. Could Alice be having an affair? The thought quickly evaporated. Tender, fulsome; we hadn't atrophied.

The next morning I was dimly aware when Alice slipped out of bed an hour before dawn. I assumed she was going to the bathroom, and didn't come fully awake for another hour. Maggie had left a note on the kitchen table:

Sorry to miss breakfast with you, Darling. My opening argument began forming in my head, couldn't wait to get to writing. In the oven there's some of that banana bread I baked last weekend. I know how much you love it. Hope your day is good. I'll probably be home pretty late tonight.

Last night was as great as ever. You haven't lost a thing. Thank you. I love you,

Alice,

Forgot to ask last night about your progress in the attic. Remember our promise to ourselves that we would finish that by summer's end.

Our selves, Alice? I don't remember being party to that promise, nor have you been a party to fulfilling it.

My petulance at Alice's perseverance didn't gain traction that morning. I was as eager as she to cull that boxful, not let Maggie eclipse the reason Alice pushed me to go up there. After a piece of the banana bread and a cup of tea, I took

Gabby for a long walk in the fresh morning air. You have a good life, Henry. Be sure to thank Alice for the spice she added to it last night.

Something pathological about feeling more comfortable with conflict than with affection. I blame Alice for being tough and preoccupied, but truth is I don't feel like I deserve a lot of affection. The Groucho Marx thing about not wanting to belong to a club that would have me for a member.

Another legacy from Maggie? You sure want her to carry your baggage, don't you, Henry?

I loved walking Gabby—feisty Norfolk terrier (named after an old boyfriend of Alice)—especially in the cemetery. The gravestones make me feel grounded. (Soon enough, Henry, don't rush it.) We'd lived in the small town for more than twenty years. I had known many of the people buried there; presided over the burial of several. Reading the names on their headstones was evocative.

Sneaks up on me how many dead people I know. How quickly and easily we get back to our lives after they die. Could be depressing, but it quite cheers me up. Love that line in Dag Hammarskjold's *Markings:* "If dying, too, is to be made a social occasion, then please let me slip out without disturbing the party." That tension, wanting to matter, and wanting to be invisible, the approach-avoidance thing can feel like my personal motto.

This stuff about our family, gentry, fomenting rabble revolution suits my passive-aggressive ambivalence. Enjoying the perks of privilege while eroding the powers that protect those perks.

A chipmunk scurried across the stone wall at the far end of the cemetery. Gabby saw it before I did, nearly jerked the leash out of my hand.

Weird, walking around these graves without terrible grief, many people I connected with, some recently dead. Yet my knees go wobbly when I walk past the grape arbor where we buried Jasmine, our Siamese cat, several years ago. Animals love without a lot of fuss. Wish Gabby would outlive me: means I'd probably have to die in the next five years.

Hmm, five years; doesn't seem so bad. I wonder if Maggie knows when I'll die?

After lunch I paid bills that had been sitting on my desk for as long as I dared wait without risking finance charges. The surprisingly nice clergy pension, plus Alice bringing in the big bucks, hadn't broken me of the habit from our early years of near poverty, doing triage with the bills, paying some right away, letting others wait.

I'd talked with Maggie about my money fetish, nearly as powerful and mysterious as God and sex.

Filthy Lucre

As I'd reached into the box for Maggie's book that afternoon, I was thinking about my preoccupation with money. Why still, now, when we had plenty?

Maggie's laugh. "You really want to do money, dear boy? It won't make you feel any more settled. If it's any comfort, money issues are a family fetish that long predates you."

I fingered the C/D tab. "de Murias, Douglas Ave., Babylon, NY."

"I regret you didn't know your cousins better, Henry. They were wonderful, full of fun. But your father worried about the influence they might have on you. Especially about money."

"How so, Maggie?"

"They had been powerful people in Havana. By pure coincidence, your father was born in the same city, into rather more modest gentility—and Gentile-ity"—Maggie's laughter at her own joke set off one of her coughing fits I remembered, caused by her heavy smoking.

"Jesus, Maggie, that cough, even when you're dead? Don't tell me you still smoke after you're dead."

As a kid I'd track her through the house by that wheezing cough. She caught her breath, sighed: "Smoking is among the mysteries that remain buried until you are, Henry.

"Dear boy, do you remember Ben's story about going to boarding school on scholarship, then Yale, where his last semester he screwed up, lost his scholarship? And his tuition was picked up by one of his father's prep school classmates, who in a gesture of huge kindness, bought his stamp collection for exactly the amount of his tuition?"

How could I forget? He repeated that story many times, as a warning against slacking off. He once admitted he got his job with Procter & Gamble thanks to that same guy, a member of the Procter family.

"Well, Ramon and his sister Angel were of a different caste from the Simpsons. Not wildly rich, but with a sense of ease about their station that made Ben envious. He worried if you hung around them, that ease about money might rub off on you. He felt I had been infected by my family's inherited money. He believed children raised with money were lazy, which he regarded as my fatal flaw. It also made him suspicious of the de Murias' politics."

"Their politics? Why, Maggie?"

"Ben was brand loyal, a company man, a corporate soldier. And a devout capitalist. He drank nasty Narragansett Beer because they sponsored the Red Sox on TV. He watched the Red Sox, so he felt obliged to drink their beer. The free market thing.

"He considered the de Murias family unprincipled,

working against not only their own government, but against their own best interests. His free-market conviction was no one acts against self-interest unless they are stupid, or driven by dangerous ideology."

I pictured Ramon, and his beautiful French wife Vivian. I met them a handful of times, the last time when I was in college. I lusted after my aunt's dazzling beauty. Envied Ramon's savoir faire. They seemed so at home with themselves. Quite different from how I felt. Ben drilled into me that I had not been to the manor born: "Nothing will be given to you, Son." How come he always called me Son when he wanted me to be aware of his authority? "You'll have to earn your own way or your life will be a disaster."

"It made Ben edgy to be around Ramon," Maggie went on. "He thought Ramon had been handed what Ben believed he had earned by the sweat of his brow."

I laughed. "You mean like how hard he sweat to earn his entre with the Procters, and a decent job during the Depression?"

Long silence. "You still there, Maggie?" Her silences often signaled something heavy in the offing.

"I was reliving something, Henry, a conversation at our dinner table in Charleston. You and your sisters had been sent upstairs to do your homework. Ben and I were discussing the note you'd brought home from your teacher. She'd written that you were slow catching on to basic Arithmetic. Must have been about third grade."

"Oh yeah, times tables." Fifty years later the memory remained clear. "I was terrified I wasn't getting that because I was just plain stupid."

Another silence—was she uncertain about showing me this? Maggie's voice became soft, cautious. "Henry, you want to be privy to that conversation? It's heavy, surprisingly still, for me. Packed with clues, maybe more than you want."

"Jesus, Maggie, sounds scary."

"It is, dear boy. Long time ago. No shame if we skip it."

Dilemma. Hate admitting I'm scared of anything. Sometimes my false bravado has led me places I wished I hadn't gone. Sweaty times, but I survived.

"What the hell, Maggie, in for a penny, in for a pound," I said, with more conviction than I felt. Stuffy attic. I peeled off my sweater. More than the temperature was making me sweat.

The dining room in our house in Charleston, 1949, matched my memory. Except for that portrait on the wall behind Ben's place. Obviously an ancestor. What ever happened to that portrait? A de Murias? Did he make Maggie get rid of it?

My parents, at opposite ends of the long mahogany table. My place, to Maggie's right and Ben's left, Victoria and Jean's places across from mine, all three empty. Dessert bowls—oh, for Christ's sweet sake, those are *finger bowls*!—linen place mats. Gertrude, gray uniform, white apron, came through the swinging door from the kitchen, cleared the bowls. I had a surge of affection seeing Gertie. Her ample lap where she'd held me when Birdie was killed.

Ben, tweed jacket, rep tie, flannel pants, dinner dress, after shedding the day's business suit. Maggie, modestly pretty, decades younger than I was now, in a brightly colored frock. Each nursed a highball glass, deep brown color, drink of choice—double bourbon—before dinner, during dinner, after dinner nightcap. Pre-wine-days, a double shot, Early Times. How could they sit up, let alone converse?

"And just what do you make of this note, Margaret?" Ben's stern—surprisingly sober—voice. A rhetorical question, no response expected, nor would one be brooked.

In present attic-time, Maggie's hoarse laugh. "You're dead right about *that*, Henry! Ben never asked a question at our dinner table that he hadn't answered in his own mind. And he expected agreemen. If you can still your heart long enough to take this in, we can talk later about what you see and hear."

The 1949 dining room. "What I make of it, Ben, is that Henry's no better at arithmetic than I am. Let's hope he doesn't have dreams of becoming an accountant."

The disgusted look on Ben's face would stop a clock.

"I expected you would make light of this, Margaret, coming from a family in which life was effortless, secure, regardless of whether you got a good education or were willing to work hard. Simpsons are not faded Spanish royalty, Margaret, and Henry's not going to be able to compensate for his deficits by marrying someone rich who will cover for him."

I winced. Shit, Ben, that was a low blow!

"Ben, Henry is nine years old."

I can't believe you let that one pass, Maggie?

"I suppose you're looking for me to apologize for whatever part of me he may have inherited that might have diluted your prized work ethic. Might you take some comfort considering Ramon—my lineage—President of Pan American Airways? You may consider the de Muriases royal no-goods, but most of us have somehow managed to make our way in the world pretty well, some quite handsomely."

"God damn it, Margaret!" Ben slammed his fist on the table, rattling the china and glasses. "Henry is a middle class American boy, not a son of faded Latin nobility, with his way forward neatly laid out for him. Someday, God willing, he'll be a man, with responsibilities, required to compete in a business jungle where the strong eat the weak for lunch. Is that what you want for your son—to become his tougher, smarter rivals' lunch?"

I watched, mesmerized. Maggie stared down the table at Ben, in silence, watching him smolder. Are you counting, Maggie, to keep from exploding?

"Whether you are aware of it, Ben, even at his young age, Henry is a gifted writer. I don't suppose you've read the poems he's been writing in Sunday School? Mrs. Kendrick was so impressed she collected them and put them into that folder he brought home a couple of weeks ago. Have you looked at them?"

Ben's expression might make you think he smelled something foul. "Looked at poems Henry wrote in Sunday School? No, Margaret, I haven't looked at them. I have no intention of looking at them. This is what is so enraging— you, and Mrs. whatever-her-name encouraging distractions Henry chooses to avoid the assigned task."

Maggie has to be steaming mad, but her appearance doesn't betray it. "So tell me, Ben," her voice dripped with sarcasm, "do you consider running Pan American Airways, the largest airline in the world, real, hard work?"

"Oh, for Christ's sake, Margaret, your cousin was born

with connections in international business that greased the skids for him at every turn. Henry is going to have to fight for everything he gets."

Hit him with the stuff about the Procters giving him his start at Procter & Gamble, Maggie! She didn't. They sat in stony silence as Gertrude cleared their places.

"We'll have coffee in the den, Gertrude," my father said, in his stern, master's voice. They rose from the table and went into the den, Ben a step ahead of Maggie. They sat, Ben picked up the newspaper. Maggie opened the New Yorker. So that's what people did before TV. How could they read after the volume of Bourbon they'd consumed?

My heart raced; beads of sweat popped out on my forehead. My parents sat by the fire in their movie-set living room, in stony silence. Gertrude brought demitasse cups on a silver tray, first to my mother, seated in the blue Queen Anne chair by the fireplace, then to my father in the wing chair with the wooden magazine rack beside it. "Thank you, Gertrude," he said, after taking sugar and cream from the tray, spooning it into his cup, while Gertrude stood beside his chair. "We won't be needing anything more tonight. We'll carry these things to the kitchen before we go upstairs."

"Yes sir, thank you, Sir. Good night. Good night, Mrs. Simpson."

Was that a conspiratorial glance that passed between Maggie and Gertrude, as Gertrude looked over her shoulder as she left the room?

"Good night, Gertrude," Maggie said, in her warmest voice, "sleep well."

A subtle smile on Gertrude's face, hidden from Ben's view by the elephant ear of the wing chair.

"Thank you, Mam, I hope the same for you."

My parents read for several minutes in silence, then Ben folded his paper, slotted it into the magazine rack beside him. He looked at his wife as if waiting for her to acknowledge that he was ready to reclaim her attention. She continued reading her New Yorker, seemingly unaware of him looking at her.

You knew damn well he was waiting for you to look up, didn't you, Maggie?

"Margaret, we can't just let this matter slide, as if it makes no difference whether Henry gets a decent education."

"Ben, he's nine years old, in third grade. It doesn't take a mother who loves him to see he's a very bright boy, finding his way perfectly well, exactly as a boy his age should be."

"Easy enough for you to say, Margaret, since your bread and butter never depended on wiles, or hard work. Tempting to dismiss it because he's still young. Before you know it he'll be old enough for boarding school, then college. By then, Margaret, game over. And our son's fate is sealed."

My anxiety was making my ears ring. My parents taking opposing sides of the battle that had raged in me, about myself, as far back as I could remember. I never knew Maggie—or anyone else—took my side, the side I wished I dared take for myself.

"So what do you propose, Ben?"

Did you have to give in so easily, Maggie?

"That we send him up to my brother's in New York, run him through those tests Harry designed for under-achievers.

Maybe they'll find something that needs medical attention, or can provide advice for getting this boy motivated."

So that's how I ended up going to New York for those three days of ridiculous tests. As it turned out, maybe not so ridiculous. I couldn't contain myself, too agitated to watch in silence any longer, I spoke to Maggie:

"I was surprised—delighted, Maggie—when you told me my IQ was 138—damn high. A lot higher than I imagined."

"You may have been delighted, dear boy, but your father wasn't. Not because I told you your IQ—I never revealed I had done that—but because it confirmed his conviction that you were lazy. And I don't think he enjoyed knowing your IQ was several points higher than his."

Oh, nasty delight!. "I never knew that. When you told me my IQ, I was glad to know I wasn't stupid. But then I worried maybe Ben was right, that my miserable performance in school was because I was lazy."

"And? What do you think about that now, Henry?"

"Differently, Maggie, though there are still days when that painful mystery about why it seems safer for me to fold under pressure haunts me. I still tend to think everyone in the room is smarter, tougher, better endowed. I mostly keep my pants on in locker rooms."

Laughter. "Sorry to say you got that performance fear from me, Henry. Good thing you were a boy, male all the way through. Have to give Ben some credit for understanding the need for a boy to learn to deal with pressure. White middle-class men were still expected to run the show. I knew you would have preferred to skip the fray, but you steeled yourself, managed it pretty well. Be nice if you could let yourself enjoy your successes, not consider them lucky accidents. Did you at least suspect you had pretty robust intellect, and competitive horsepower, even during those years you were failing in school?"

I had no ready answer, not sure even now that I trust my smarts. When I revisit those years, my anxiety can block out everything except the fear.

"You're one smart cookie, Maggie, Must have killed you to watch me flailing, knowing what you knew. I can't say my successes have ever totally erased the fear. When Alice fixes me with that cross-examining glare, I see Ben, and retreat into that dysfunctional boy."

Maggie's laughter at this was augmented by the uproar of the Canada geese's territorial battle on the pond below. Take a step back, Henry, it *is* funny, you and Alice doing your primal, territorial dance. You'd think thirty-plus years would help you be beyond Ben's intimidation. And all that pastoral counseling you did, with some pretty screwy couples. You often suggested that marriage, when it works, is more sport than the fairy tale it's portrayed as.

As for Ben and my IQ, those smarts have served you pretty well. So Ben didn't dig your poetry; he was in awe of that big parish that chose you as rector.

"Heavy stuff, Maggie. I'm ready for some time to reflect—and for an armful of paper to buy off Alice. Thanks for a wild, entertaining morning."

Must be the way of the dead. Silence. Not just silence, dead air. We're done; Maggie's gone. Without comment. What determines the tenure of a relationship with a dead person?

Whatever, she was gone. The air in the attic changes, when she comes and when she leaves. Spooky.

With considerable self-congratulation I carried an armful of exam blue books down to the garage. The volume of throwaway, not revelations from my late mother, would be Alice's measure of how useful today's time in the attic was.

They say every man marries his mother; I got that a little skewed, married my father. Or assigned Alice the role I'd assigned him: rooting me out of my psychic torpor often enough to accomplish a few chores, rather than spending my entire time massaging the ineffable. I'm still as petulant with Alice as I had been with Ben for relentlessly keeping me on task. And once the task is accomplished, just as grateful even if I felt bullied into it.

Gabby met me at the foot of the attic stairs, tail wagging, eyes fixed on me, expectantly.

"Gabby, I once thought God would explain all this to me one day if I was faithful and patient enough. Maybe God would have, if I had been patient and faithful. Thanks to you I don't have to wait for God.

"Alice keeps me attached to the earth, even still sleeps with me, after thirty-plus years. Such dumb luck. Makes a shitload of money, too. Doing stuff she loves and I'd hate. What a deal!

"And you, Gabby, you listen to me, lead me through the graveyard, woods, never lose patience with my wandering. Man's best friend's too tame; you're this man's alter ego."

I suppose it's bogus to ascribe human feelings to dogs, but I do. I knew Gabby loved when I talked to him like that. Wagged his tail, whimpering empathy, loves my weirdness, never calls me an asshole. All this in return for a few friskies and a warm place to sleep.

"Let's take a walk, boy, I want to tell you about something that came to me when Maggie was showing me my ancestors on that balcony in Havana. About working both sides of the street. You'll be fascinated."

Gabby wagged his tail, stretched, and went to the door, while I put a few friskies in my pocket and picked up a shit mitt. "It's not that long a story; it'll take us around the cemetery and back." Gabby pawed at the door.

"Have I told you that Alice and I were at Richard Nixon's second inauguration in 1973? Had a spot on the reviewing stand in front of the White House? Danced the night away at the inaugural ball? That I beat Jeb Magruder, playing tennis on the White House court? Yes, *that* Jeb Magruder, who did jail time for Watergate.

"Did I mention marching on the Pentagon after Nixon's Christmas bombing of Hanoi? And the very next day having lunch in the White House mess with friends, Nixon's spear-carriers? Sound like our ancestors watching Estrada's inaugural parade?

⌣

"I don't mind telling you, Gabby, it made my head spin. Jeb Magruder, right after getting out of jail, visited me to unwind for a while. I'd moved to a new parish by then.

"He agreed to speak to a group of my parishioners, who of course thought he'd been persecuted for being one of them. His record as a Watergate felon marked him a steadfast Nixon man, enhancing my Republican parishioners' admiration. Reassured them that Magruder was my friend—and he was, good friend, whom I liked, good tennis player—maybe I wasn't the misguided radical they sometimes worried I was. Oh God, I felt like a whore. Talk about working both sides of the street.

"Magruder's exchange with those parishioners, when one of them asked him how a nice young man like him got himself into such a mess, still echoes in my head.

"'Do you think your Rector is a man of integrity?' 'Jesus, Magruder, give it a rest. They all nod. Whew. 'Well, he made no secret he disapproved of our administration, marched against the war, scorned our so-called Southern Strategy, called it thinly disguised racism. But, you know, I don't recall his ever turning down a chance to play tennis on the White House court, or have lunch in the White House mess. Hard to understand if you haven't been there.'

"Guffaws from my parishioners. I'm usually loathe to admit I've ended up among my people: sophisticated, accepting of life's ambiguities. Instinctive agnostics. I'm sure this unprincipled dimension in me—exposing my clay feet to people who heard me preach every week—raised me a notch in their eyes. At least increased my likeability. And confirmed my feeling like a whore, pimping for a god they didn't really believed in, but thought I ought to."

"So what do you think about that, Gabby? Pretty sordid, huh? Make you disappointed in your old man?"

Gabby had sat patiently through my monologue. He looked up at me, yawned.

"A brave colleague once said, during a heated debate about how the shrinking Episcopal Church might flourish again, the way the fundamentalist, born-again churches then were, 'The Episcopal Church needs to regain the courage of her confusion.' The hall erupted in laughter. He'd said something sort of scandalous, accurately describing why the Episcopal Church was a Dodo bird, headed for extinction, in a culture that mistrusts ambiguity.

"And portrayed our stark choice: feed our envy of those churches' growing numbers, trash our historical ethos, pretend certainty, or watch our numbers fall. The church and I did both, and neither, never really made the choice.

"You want to know the most scandalous part, Gabby?" His expression assured me he was eager to hear it. "I love the courage of our confusion thing. It didn't make for growth in the parishes I worked in, but it beat the hell out of pretending to know what God was up to. Or that the god we prayed to was anything more than a projection of the wishes we couldn't fulfill for ourselves."

Gabby stood and shook, as if he'd just had a bath. "That's right, big guy, if they don't get it, shake off the dust and move on."

Pumped from having Gabby listen so patiently and without judgment, to a story that once made me feel terrible about myself, I went to the attic, persuaded I'd shored up my sense of myself, ready for more Maggie.

The Bishop

"ODDLY ENOUGH," Maggie, as usual, began without introduction, "this also took place in the Caribbean, Puerto Rico, not Cuba, many years later, when Puerto Rico was an American territory. Your grandfather, Ben's father, had gone from Pulaski, Tennessee, where he spent his deacon year after seminary, to be Dean of the Episcopal Cathedral in Havana right after he was ordained priest. He can't have been more than twenty-five. Maybe something to do with his older brother who went there after medical school to do his residency. Why Havana remains a mystery.

"Ben was born there, and a couple of years later, your grandfather was made Bishop of Puerto Rico and the American Virgin Islands. In those days missionary bishops were appointed by the House of Bishops, not elected by members of the diocese. So he likely went without anyone there knowing him, and without his knowing much about his new diocese.

"What you're going to see now took place in San Juan when they had lived there for several years."

I saw Graddy and our Aunt Sally, on opposite sides of the dining room table. They're facing each other, their faces grim.

"'See that, Henry?" Maggie asked, "You never knew your grandfather as a young man. Handsome, isn't he?" And I had no idea how beautiful Sally was. "Now listen in."

"Oh, Sally, Sally," Graddy's strong, baritone voice was evocative—a preacher's voice more than a daddy's—"how could you have let this happen? I'm at a loss for words to express the depth of my disappointment in you."

Ooh, that shaming voice. Now you know where Ben learned to speak like that. Made my stomach churn. But apparently not Sally's. She looked across the table at him, her chin thrust forward defiantly.

"*Let* it happen, Daddy? I didn't *let* it happen; I *prayed* it would happen."

Graddy's head fell forward, abjectly. He slowly looked up, across the table at her, his eyes narrowed, his breakfast untouched. "Sally, oh my dear daughter, it was only with the greatest reluctance I gave you my blessing after you insisted you were going to get married when you were only 17 years old. But this…"

Sally's expression grew even more fierce. "Your *blessing*, Daddy? You call that half-assed OK you gave us, when I told you we were going to run off to a state that didn't require parents' permission, a blessing? Is that the kind of niggardly blessing you offer your adoring flock?"

Graddy half rose from his chair, as if he might lean across

the table and hit her, then seemed to think better of it, settled back. "You're speaking to your father, young lady, and I'll thank you to show proper respect."

Sally slumped down in her chair, the fight seeming to drain from her. "I meant no disrespect, Daddy, it's just that I need your help. If you won't help me, I'm going to be in worse trouble than you can imagine."

"Let me be sure I fully understand, Sally. You're married to Frank, but you're carrying his brother Cliff's baby. Is that right?"

"Yes."

"And you're asking me to help you divorce Frank and marry Cliff; do I have that right?"

"Yes."

I hardly dared take a breath.

Sally and Graddy studied each other's faces. Finally he spoke. "Would it be too much to ask how you got yourself into this fix? I mean what, besides teenage lust—my own daughter's animal lust—could have led you to such a shameful thing?"

I was glued to the scene. This was our Aunt Sally, our father's oldest sister, whom I had considered the family matriarch. I loved her, even though she seemed a little stuck up, painfully proper. Fact is, I was kind of scared of her.

"I'll tell you this much, Daddy," Sally said. "Frank was wonderful when we were courting. I was excited about life on the farm. But the day after our wedding, he turned into a tyrant. He made it clear he considered his wife just another farmhand. When I balked at cleaning out the horse stalls—Daddy, you know I was brought up to be a lady, not a farmhand"—for the first time Sally's emotion showed, though she only whimpered—"Frank beat me up."

Graddy's eyes widened, his head snapped forward. "He *beat* you? Your husband *beat* you?"

Sally's defiance evaporated. The tear rolling down her cheek was answer enough to her father's question.

"Why didn't you tell me, Sally?"

"Oh, I wanted to, Daddy, but I was ashamed. I thought it was my fault. Frank was my husband. It embarrassed me that he was disappointed I wasn't a better wife. I thought if I worked harder I'd get better at it, and then he would treat me better. But pretty soon it was happening every day."

"Every *day*? Oh Sally!" He reached across and covered her hand with his. Graddy's eyes filled, something I never remember seeing. Sally sobbed. He held her hand until her crying slowed. "And Cliff, Sally? Can you tell me how that terrible business with Frank ended up with you getting pregnant with Cliff's child? And, please, spare me the details."

Sally actually laughed through her tears at her father's pious sensibility. Tough woman, that one. Her face was crimson; snot dripping from her nose. My heart ached with love for her. What a fucking mess, and she still had the strength to find her father's delicate feelings funny.

"Oh Daddy, Cliff knew his brother better than I did. He knew what was likely to happen once we were married. He started coming out to the farm every couple of days just to check on me. The first few times I greeted him cheerfully, lied, said everything was fine. Then one day he saw the bruises on my arm and face, and he knew. No details, Daddy, but I was all too eager to fall into his comforting arms."

My eyes filled as I saw our grandfather's fill again.

"So, Henry," Maggie's voice brought me back to the stuffy attic, "that's the F. C. Adams family. Cliff and Sally Adams. Sally married her brother-in-law, Cliff. These are your ancestors on Ben's strait-laced, Anglo side. The squared-away, exemplary bunch that Ben held up as icons. Not like the decadent, Hispanic, de Murias group."

I took a deep breath. The story wiped me out. "So our cousin Althea is really Frank's daughter, not Cliff's?

Holy shit, you couldn't make this stuff up. It must have killed Graddy."

"I suppose," Maggie said, "if you think biology decides these things, yes, Althea was Frank's daughter, not Cliff's. But in every way that counts, Cliff was her dad, as we always believed. I have no idea whether Althea even knows all this. And, if you can believe it, there's more to the story, maybe even more compelling, if you're interested."

"*Interested*? I'm spellbound."

"Remember," she continued, "Graddy had been in the Caribbean for a while by then. The Latin culture had weaned him, at least some, from his southern pieties. And maybe this experience with Sally helped move him from conventional guardian of the status quo to supporter of the downtrodden, which is where he ended up."

"Doesn't sound like the strait-laced, tight-assed Graddy I remember."

"Yeah, well you were a kid, remember. Kids are often surprised to discover the radicals hidden under their parents' conventional skin."

Jesus, truer words were never spoken.

"Remember that picture of the cathedral in San Juan. What you're about to be privy to took place in his office there a couple of hours before the exchange you just saw between your grandfather and Sally. Sally didn't know about the earlier exchange.

Simply furnished. Prayer desk in the corner. Did he actually use it? I had one in my office, used it a few times, when the shit was hitting the fan. His cluttered desk, a chair a couple of feet in front of his desk, where supplicants sat to beg him for divine favor.

"Hope you understand, Henry, that unkind thought about begging for favor was yours, not Graddy's."

OK, Maggie, OK.

Granny was standing in front of his desk while Graddy sat in his high, lattice-back, throne-chair, behind it. He looked surprised, none too happy to have to look up to her. She hadn't told him she was coming, had brushed by his secretary who guarded his office like a sentry. Granny told him the sad story Sally had told to her earlier. Her face was resolute, an expression I don't remember seeing on her.

Here's how the conversation went...

Granny was speaking, ignoring his frequent attempts to interrupt and retake the floor from her. Graddy made one grand attempt to regain control: "Sarah, I am the Bishop; it won't do for the Bishop's daughter to be seen as some common slut."

At the word slut, Granny's back stiffened under her gingham sundress. "Charles, I wouldn't care if you were Almighty God, Himself." Ooh, that made him flinch! "This is your *child*, our flesh and blood, not some slut, as you just called her. Not one of your flock you can cast out by your divine prerogative. I'm tempted to shame you, reminding you that our Lord Himself was born to an unmarried mother. I'll spare you that." She'd hardly spared him. "But you are going to listen to her, and then we're going to help her through this in whatever way she needs."

Graddy's eyes flashed angrily. "Sarah Palmer"—had he ever called her out like that before, evoking her maiden name?—"you listen to me…"

"No, not this time, Charles," she interrupted—I don't think he was used to being interrupted by anyone—"this time you're going to listen to *me*. Our first-born daughter is in trouble, and we're going to help her. That's the end of this matter."

She turned on her heel and stalked out of his office.

He came home an hour later. That's when he and Sally had the conversation we saw earlier. I understood he preserved a modicum of his dignity by acting incredulous, indignant, as if this was the first he'd heard of it.

My grandfather, a cleric of the old school, member of the power elite. It cheers me up, reassures me, seeing him swallow his principles to help out his daughter. And how about mushy old Granny being the one who browbeat him into it?

"Faced with his frightened daughter," Maggie said, "when he understood the whole story, Sally was not only his beloved daughter, but a young girl cruelly hurt by arbitrary authority. For your grandfather, the unfairness of her predicament trumped even the rigid rules of male ecclesiastical hierarchy he considered inviolable."

Another notch in that belt, marking things changing in ways I could never have imagined.

"You know, Maggie, those old rules, maybe a tad more relaxed, were still largely in place when I started seminary. In those three short years—1963 to 1966—they took a beating none of us saw coming. I was a fully formed adult by then, and, though there was much about the old ways I found oppressive, that world was imbedded in my bones. In my head I understood how quickly and wholesale the old ways were being challenged. I was happy to see them lose their hold, but I don't think they can ever fully displace the old ones lodged in my bones.

"And Granny; I'd never have recognized in that fierce woman the frumpy lady I remember vegetating in her old age."

"I understand that you had already been largely formed when the ground began shifting, but if you succumb to the fear that rouses in you, you miss so much, Henry.

"Do you remember where your grandmother grew up?"

"Florida, right? Fernandina Beach, I think. I went there once, asked in the town office if I could look at some of their records from when she was a girl. They'd had a fire destroy everything before 1940."

"Too bad. Any idea, Henry, where Jose Marti spent his exile before he returned to try to overthrow Spanish rule in Cuba?"

"Seriously, Maggie?"

"Right, Fernandina Beach. Marti was an intellectual, a poet really, more than a revolutionary. He used to spend mornings at the Palmer house writing poetry. Took a shine to your grandmother who was just a little girl, but a precocious little girl, and he became her mentor, as a poet, and as a fearless champion of people abused by power."

"Granny and Jose Marti composed poetry together?"

"And no doubt talked about his intention to lead an uprising in Cuba."

"No shit."

"Your great grandparents lost some friends in Fernandina, who thought it was unseemly for them to hang out with Marti, not only a Cuban, but whom many considered a troublemaker. Your great grandparents even raised money for him. They tried to talk him out of going back because they didn't think he was well-suited for war. They were right. He was killed in the very first battle. Broke their hearts. And cemented convictions that set them on a course for the rest of their lives. Your grandmother's picture of the world was forged in that fire."

"And Graddy, a generation before mine, with far more at stake as a bishop than I ever had to protect as a parish priest, let go of so much he once considered inviolable… My respect for those two just ratcheted way up. Who knew?"

"Nicely put, Henry. Now maybe you won't feel you have to fend me off when I say you are their heir in ways you've never considered."

⌒

I carried an armful of old blue exam books down the stairs, pleased with myself for piling up performance points with

Alice. Peeling a hard-boiled egg for my egg-salad sandwich, my mind wandered through so many times the world I considered settled seemed to come unstuck.

A guy—what was his name? Doug, I think—forensic pathologist, gay—showed up for the Blessed Group, people with terminal diagnoses, with whom I met weekly in my last parish. His face is burned into memory.

Doug had AIDS in the days when that was a death sentence. Pathologist to his end, he regaled the group each week with a new insight gained from watching the disease progress and his body diminish. Some in the group found it hard at first to listen to his clinical description of his own impending death. Eventually his humor and clinical fearlessness won us over.

A month or so before he died, Doug told us that he was practicing dying. He would lie on his back in bed before going to sleep and imagine letting parts of himself go: first his feet, then his legs, and so on. Once I asked how far he'd gotten. He smiled, said he'd thought he'd made it all the way up to his waist, but then noticed his toes were twitching, so he began over again.

I was with him when he died. Risky as it is to try to interpret what's going on with someone when they're no longer able to communicate, their consciousness receded beyond reach, Doug appeared to die as he intended, quietly, gently. An hour before he stopped breathing, he opened his eyes for a moment, seemed to see me, murmured, "Oh," smiled, and returned to wherever he had been, on his way to wherever he was going. I've tried practicing dying a few times when I couldn't fall asleep. Not much good at it. Yet.

Shortly after Doug died I wrote this poem.

Dead Serious

He'd had, he said,
a rollicking affair
with death
playing
dead
he'd stretch out solemn
still
soft focusing his eyes so they stared without
seeing
He'd like you to think he found it
funny
teasing death
but like some other slices
of his life
he wished us to suppose
he could be cavalier about,
about dying he was surprisingly
serious
dead serious.

My fascination with death was a source of amusement among some parishioners, troubling to others. Henry the "death man" didn't particularly amuse my family. One summer, when I was on vacation, a young parishioner turned suddenly sick, seemingly unto death. Her mother expressed her fright to a friend who said, "Not to worry; Henry's on vacation; people can die only when he's on duty." Sure enough, the girl recovered, and my dubious reputation grew.

I see dying as a very big deal, for everyone, regardless of what they've been taught or think they believe. Right up there with the mystery of being born from what seems nearly nothing. Our choice being between trying to face it openly, consciously, or obliquely, unconsciously, in the shadows. Where fear rules. But face it we will, as surely as our baby teeth fall out to make way for adult teeth.

The attic conversations with Maggie—fantasy, projection, unnamable spirit visit,—upped the ante for me. Not only because she was dead, but because she'd kicked over the props that had concealed her from me when she was alive.

"God damn it, Henry," Alice said, "who are you trying to fool, that you're not scared to die, just like everyone?"

Being present for many people's deaths strengthened my conviction (hope?) that dying—as mysterious and challenging as being born—is, finally, ecstasy. But I hadn't died, had only watched others die. So I had to give Alice her due.

"Yes, it scares me, Alice. Being born must be pretty scary, having to leave that snug, warm, safe place. It's not about getting rid of the fear. Being afraid to die makes us creative rather than passive. It's about whether the pain of birth, and the angst of death, rob being here of its value. Has the thrill of being here outweighed the sorrows, made the risk of loving, knowing how it has to come out, made life seem like a good bet? Or cruel joke?"

Alice, the hardheaded lawyer, wants the whole package: "What about life after death? Is this *it*?"

"Maybe, who knows? But is life cool enough, what we can know of it, that you're willing trust the rest, even the dying?"

"I could so easily destroy you on the witness stand, Henry. None of that spooky shit would stand up in court."

"Likely not, Alice. Guess we'll have to wait to see how it holds up."

After one of those exchanges, I wrote this poem. My editor went for it. I didn't show it to Alice. Maybe she'll read it someday.

Quarter Hour

Last night's
dream
probed an old awe.

I'd been sentenced to
death
for what I don't know
(but you who know me will understand when I say it
    was no injustice)

I was being led to the execution chamber by a dispas-
     sionate
guard
Alice walked alongside
her affect resolute
I would have thought I'd want her to seem more
distressed
but instead I felt oddly comforted by her
intrepid
restrained compassion

We three walked the hall in silence until I asked,
"When we reach the chamber, can you say how long it
     will be
until…
(I recall a big pause here)
the lethal injection?"
"15 minutes," he said, with no
hesitation
I wished I hadn't asked, or he hadn't answered so
certainly

Now I knew without
doubt
in ¼ hour after we got there I'd be
dead.

My heart pounded, I felt the
blood
rush to my face

Would my knees buckle?
Alice let me spend the weighty moment
then took my hand but the familiar feel of her warm
flesh
was eclipsed by an ancient issue, whether it's okay
to die
when it's time

Whether what sprung from
seeming stillness
a scant six decades
ago
can be counted on to conduct
a quickened quark
to its succeeding
station

Has this dream sprung from my fecund
prayers   for
Love
     money

        time
   health
all leaving me at last with

            me?

Wherever you go, promised the Zen master,
there you

          are

Dreams dreamed, miraculously,
savored,
turn over
ground
left untilled until
the garden's guardian   sword aflame
unearths the answer as if you seriously meant to ask
the question

15 minutes.

Okay, madam editor, that's the final word on Quarter Hour. You made me rewrite it a hundred times. Huge relief, finally closing the books on a piece—maybe dying is like that—feeling accomplished, OK, done. Alice will be home soon; she'll ask what I've done all day.

"You spent the whole day on two poems, Henry? And no doubt they're both about dying." "No, Babe," I respond in my imagination, "Check out all the stuff in the trash I took out of the box today. And I did have a brief exchange with Minnie Stetson as I stood on her grave after texting my dear friend Alfred who had mostly disappeared from my life."

Aaron's Blessing

IT'S UNDENIABLE THAT DEATH seems to follow me around like a domesticated animal. Or feral beast. As if it picks up my scent.

Gabby met me at the foot of the stairs, wagging his tail, barking impatiently. I scooped a cup of friskies into his bowl; he gobbled it in fifteen seconds. Sated, he went to his cushion, sat quietly, attentive.

"Gabby, I'm so glad I don't feel like I need to hide from you. You don't care whether I believe in God or can make sense of what that has to do with being a priest. Or maybe you're just too kind to say so. You respect me even when I kiss rich people's asses.

"Are you embarrassed that I don't push back harder against Alice's lawyerly aggressiveness?

"Or surprised that Maggie turns out to have been a force, despite being belittled in our family?

"Maybe you always knew that priest chose me more than

I chose priest. That ordination was the best I could come up with to house my passions and convictions and still have a shot at a legitimate place in this world.

"You always knew, didn't you, Gabby, that Alice respects my vocation as much as I do hers? That I project onto her that she makes shit of my arcane vocation because I think that may spare me the pain of thinking that about myself."

Gabby rolled his head side to side, a gesture I love, his supportive response. He whined, scratched my leg with his paw, reassuring me: "Yeah, Henry, you're just fine. Now, how about we go out for a pee and some sniffing."

"You're the best, Gabby. You put up with my manic attempts to unpack mystery: money, sex, lame jokes, God, climate warming. You're all the company a body could ask in the fruitless pursuit of salvation."

Reassured that we were on good terms, Gabby waited by the door as I attached his leash and put on my walking shoes.

We diverted from our usual route. The previous day's rain would have made our favorite path through the cemetery muddy. This route took us through the village center where we could greet the couple who run the grocery store, maybe catch a little of the shenanigans always in play among the tattooed kids who worked at the gas station. I imagined Gabby preferred the walk through the cemetery, where I'd let him off the leash to explore scents left by the rodents that burrowed down to feed on our late, composting neighbors. Bodies, ashes. I wonder if Maggie was glad she'd been cremated, become food for roses, rather than rodents? Thought you didn't believe in life after death, Henry. Yeah, but Maggie's different.

As we approached the gas station there was a crash of crunching metal as a Ford Focus sideswiped an eighteen-wheeler going the opposite direction, swerved across the road, nearly corrected, hit the guard rail. The driver's door flew open and a woman was thrown free, onto the side of the road. Gabby and I, maybe fifty yards away, sprinted toward the accident. Two people ran out of the gas station from the other side. We arrived at the same time. I knelt down next to the woman. Her eyes were closed. Not much blood, no obvious body dislocations.

I put my hand on her shoulder. She was on her side in a fetal position. "Are you OK?"

"I don't know." She was crying, but conscious. I had my left hand through Gabby's leash; he tried to lick her face before I pulled him off. "Please let him lick me," she said, "my dog would do that. I know it would help." She must not be too badly hurt. In a habitual gesture, I put my right hand on her forehead reciting the ancient Aaronic blessing:

"Unto God's gracious mercy and protection I commit you; the Lord bless you and keep you; the Lord make His face to shine upon you…"

"How did you know I was Jewish?" she interrupted.

I laughed. "Well, we Christians borrowed most of what we have from you since we swear allegiance to an ancient rabbi from Nazareth."

She laughed, winced. "Oh, that hurts."

"Broken ribs, I'd bet." I remembered, after a couple of bike crashes, how painful it was to even take a breath. "The ambulance is housed just up the road, be along any minute." The words were hardly spoken before I heard the siren.

"God love you, sweetheart," I said, "Looks like you're going to make it. But those ribs will smart for a while."

"I am so grateful you were here," she said. The paramedics unloaded the body board from the ambulance. Gabby and I slipped away.

"We make a great team in a crunch, huh Gabby." He looked up at me, his cropped tail wagging with an intensity that makes me wonder what sort of muscle must run it. "Maybe I really was in the right business."

The highs I got from those moments sometimes caused conflict with Alice. She accused me of being a disaster junkie, of being wonderful with everyone in trouble, except members of our own family. Didn't do me much good to quote that Nazarene rabbi: "A prophet is not without honor, save in his own country." I knew from conversations with colleagues it was pretty universal.

Automatically going toward what most people (whom Alice calls "normal") go out of their way to avoid, is my default instinct.

The Blessed Group again, my favorite part of the week.

Began with three people. "What are we supposed to do here?" someone asked the first meeting. "I don't know," I answered, "*die*?" Raucous laughter. By the end of the first month the group had grown to eleven. Among the new recruits were people who walked by the closed office door and hearing the uproar, asked the receptionist, "What's going on in there? They telling dirty jokes?"

"I have no idea," she answered. "All I know is they're all dying. Maybe they find that funny." Word got out. A few, eager, I guess, for someplace safe to laugh at what they thought bizarre, invented ominous prognoses for themselves to qualify for membership in the group. Several, looking for reassurance, either that they would go to heaven when they died, or that religious renewal would protect them from dying, came to one meeting and never returned.

Alice considered hilarity among dying people to be nuts. But I think the energy in my voice as I described the group trumped her distaste. "Yet one more piece of you, Henry, outside the bounds of normality. But I have to admit, you're easier to live with since you began that group."

There weren't many things I missed since stepping down from priest work, but I did miss that group.

"I know it makes you nervous, Henry," Maggie had said, "your shakiness about what Alice considers normal and why it is you feel so alive in places most people go out of their way to avoid.

"That doesn't make you crazy or neurotic. Or no crazier or more neurotic than the rest of humanity."

When Alice got home that night, I described the accident to her. "Wow, Henry, that woman was really lucky you just happened along right then. I can't imagine anyone I'd rather have show up at a moment like that than you."

"I appreciate that, Alice. I'm glad it doesn't just rev up your feelings about my being a disaster junkie."

She got up from her place at the table, came to my side and squeezed my head in a bear hug. "I'm tough on you sometimes, Henry. It surprises me you still care what I think; you're so focused when it really counts. I'm in awe of that, maybe even a little jealous. People constantly tell me how much it meant that you were there when the shit hit the fan for them. Makes me proud of my compassionate husband." She kissed the top of my head.

"You've got to stop doing that," I joked; "you're going to wear away the few hairs still left up there."

"I promise not to make it a habit."

⌒

"So tell me something, Maggie; did you ever *get it* for yourself? The way you're so graciously leading me to see it for myself? I mean your boozing, chain-smoking, reclusiveness; was that not really you, just cover for who you really were?"

Laughter. "Oh no, Henry. Don't get me wrong; I don't hold myself up as any poster girl for enlightened living. I was pretty insightful, but the train wreck you saw was the real me. I hated that you translated that to mean you were somehow destined to follow the same path. Let's keep it clear, dear boy—you invited me into this conversation, not to rewrite my history, but to claim what's rightfully yours."

Sciatic beginning to sting, early warning: running low on fuel. "Yeah, yeah, I get it,"—my sciatic ramped up my petulance—"but the boozing and lassitude? What was that about?"

More laughter. "I'm an alcoholic, Henry, the real thing. I love bourbon. I often preferred being drunk to being sober. I could see what my life would be like sober and it didn't appeal to me. People keep their distance from a drunk. I periodically considered getting sober, especially when Ben did. But booze, in addition to being my favored anesthetic, shielded me from a lot I was happy to be free of. Thank God there weren't SATs when I was a kid. You know, honestly, my drinking didn't keep me from much I cared about. With the exception of making you feel so at risk."

Burning butt, right cheek. "I'm grateful to have worked out how not to follow you there, Maggie. I understand, better than I wish, how often I would have been grateful for a happier filter than mere grim determination between me and a lot of what my life demanded."

"I know, Henry; oh don't I know. I worried that you might turn to booze to cushion yourself from that. Tricky, delicate balance, finding a place for yourself that people respect, without crushing parts of yourself you know are precious, of your essence. Speaking of crushing, you look pretty uncomfortable crushing your sciatic on that trunk. Time for a break?"

⌣

Alice got home just after seven. It was dark, chilly. Having fed and walked Gabby, put out a tray of cheese and crackers, wine glasses, made pesto to put on pasta, washed greens for a salad, set the table, and made sure I'd removed the magazines scattered around the living room, puffed up the cushions where I'd been sitting, so they looked showroom new, I admired the fruits of my marital leashing. Quite a husband, you, Henry. Still pisses me off to have to fluff up the cushions.

Hearing her car pull in, I took a deep breath, preparing

myself for Alice being too preoccupied with the day's demands to see the heroic effort I'd made.

"Oh Henry," she exclaimed as she came through the garage door, "it smells delicious! Garlic! Love the smell of garlic sautéing." She dropped her briefcase onto the floor and opened her arms, inviting me into an embrace.

Bingo! A real kiss, soft lips, full embrace, different from our usual perfunctory greeting.

"Well, today brought a brand new wrinkle," Alice said as we unwound our embrace. "You know that Wikileaks revelation about the guy at Citibank—Hugh Foster—the one who's become my client, who the State Department cable accused of helping launder Afghan drug money to take the heat off Karzai?"

I had a vague memory of something about that online yesterday. I nodded, figuring Alice would fill me in.

"Well, guess what? That poor bastard was being set up. His boss at Citi, and some guy who supposedly reported to Foster, turns out to have been on the CIA payroll. They put the squeeze on him, making it look like he was doing the dirty work on his own hook. Shameless pricks."

I knew better than to jump in. Doesn't sound much like corporate law, or anything Armstrong, Bucks, Jervis & Riggs would touch; best just listen.

"He's given us a big retainer, being supported by Act Blue. He wants to sue both the Bank and Uncle Sam. This ups the original ante in ways I figured would make the big dogs decide to take it away from me. Guess what? I got assigned the lead in the case."

"Holy shit, Alice! Are you kidding me? Do you even *want* that case? I mean Citibank, the eight-hundred-pound gorilla? Not to mention Uncle Sam himself, the fucking CIA! That's playing in some pretty heavy traffic!"

"You bet it is. And I'm hot for it. No more condescension from those fucking senior partners. I can understand why it scares you, Hank. Let's hope our tax returns are in good shape."

Oh, man, imagine choosing this. She only calls me Hank when she's manic.

"This positions us—positions me—smack in the middle of the biggest story holding the world's attention right now. The Middle East is imploding, and, thanks to those crazy-ass Wikileaks guys, we now know our government has been playing cozy with those despots we've been propping up with taxpayer money. Now they're are falling like dominoes."

Wait 'til Alexander hears about this!

"And those pricks in Washington have been cavalierly feeding our own people, like my client Hugh Foster, to the wolves. There's no depth our government won't stoop to, doing its dirty tricks. Thanks to Wikileaks and our legal system—I hope to hell our legal system still counts for something; isn't just another piece of the shell game—the free ride is over for those assholes. It's time these people were held accountable. And we're the ones who are going to do that."

It was big stuff, but it made me laugh. "My Sweet, you haven't even taken your coat off and you're delivering your opening statement to the jury. I'm ready to vote: guilty as charged. How about I take your coat, you take a hot tub, I fix you a glass of wine, and then you can fill me in on the rest?"

Alice smiled wearily. I helped her out of her coat: could feel her shoulders drop as she released the day's tension. I leaned down to fetch her briefcase.

"God, Henry, every overworked lawyer should be so lucky as to have a wife like you waiting at home."

What once would have sounded belittling now felt welcome. You like taking care of Alice. Neither of you finds it easy to let the other do that. When she shows you she appreciates it, it's like the sun coming out from behind the clouds.

Alice went into the bedroom. I heard the tub filling. I poured myself a glass of wine, checked the internet one last time (why? what am I expecting? I never buy a lottery ticket), closed down the computer, and went to the kitchen to finish preparing dinner.

Seems true, what goes around comes around. Alice being immersed in an updated American version of the kind of intrigue Maggie's family got into in Cuba. The well-born bringing down the super well-born. Lord Acton, wasn't it? Absolute power corrupts absolutely. The second-tier jumps at the chance to bring down the top tier. You have to wonder if it's just a vicious circle. Sylvia de Murias. Sarah Palmer. Alice. Our women folk, Gabby.

Washed of her day's tensions, Alice emerged famished. She dropped into the couch, nearly disappearing into the nest of down cushions, sipped the glass of Chardonnay I handed her, and sighed.

"That sigh came from somewhere way down there, Ali."

As I considered her, child-size, enveloped by pillows, my

affection for her welled up. Made me smile. No one at Armstrong, Bucks ever sees her like that. I poured her half a glass and went into the kitchen to drain the pasta, mixed in the pesto, tossed the salad, serving it onto the plates I'd warmed in the oven. What a guy, Henry!

"Thought it would be nice to eat at the dining room table tonight," I called out to her. No response. I looked over. Dead asleep, her head drooped onto her chest. I reached down, touching her shoulder. "Ali, let's get a little dinner in you, then off to bed."

She opened her eyes, struggling to focus. "Oh, Henry, I'm so sorry. You've fixed a perfect dinner. I do need to eat. The table looks lovely."

We ate mostly in silence, broken by Alice's occasional sighs, to which I responded with reassuring murmurs. I brought coffee after clearing the table. I relished Alice's unusual vulnerability. Exhausted though I knew she was, I had one more thing up my sleeve.

I put on music I had downloaded onto the iPod that morning. Alice perked up as the music began.

"Is that what I think it is, Henry?"

"If you're thinking Bernstein's MASS, it is."

Such a happy smile.

"You finally actually found it. Oh, Henry, thank you! I have been wanting to hear it ever since I read that review in The New York Review of Books. Hard to remember what bad reviews it got when it was first performed for the opening of the Kennedy Center."

We listened, occasionally commenting about what a period piece it was—laughing when Bernstein shifted musical genres, not bothering with a transition. On the couch, thighs and shoulders gently brushing, we listened to the more than two hours of the piece, I occasionally reaching up over to massage her neck. Alice closed her eyes, sighing, leaning into me. The MASS ended (Ita Missa Est). I turned toward Alice, kissed her full on the mouth, softly, and when she responded, more firmly, parting my lips, delighted she offered her tongue in response.

I touched her breast.

"Henry! Here?"

"Why not?"

Alice smiled, ran her hand up my thigh.

Except for diminished agility, peeling clothing, demanding contortions from no-longer-limber bodies, it seemed almost like courting days. Except, Henry, this time it was your initiative.

The outcome was nearly as explosive as back then.

Spent, we lay in an awkward snarl of discarded clothing, our protesting muscles insisting we untangle before our muscles seized up. No savoring, napping, as we once did. We began to laugh.

"Guess we're not dead yet, huh, Henry?"

"Dead? Hardly. You haven't lost anything, Alice; still the sexiest woman on the planet."

"And you, Henry, you old stud. Who needs Viagra?"

"Not with a siren like you!"

Spent, we headed for bed, finessing brushing, flossing, lotion rubs, Lipitor, Ibuprofen, dropped our clothes onto a chair, and fell into bed. We slept soundly, legs and arms curled around each other. When was the last time we had gone through the night without Alice poking me to change position to stop my snoring?

In the morning, ingénue Alice was again lawyer Alice, hurrying through breakfast, focused on her iPhone. My warmth for her wasn't the least diminished by her return to her brusque persona. Sobering how much her affection, or withholding of it, can color my day. Today was going to be a happy, productive day. I wasn't quick enough to send her off with the long embrace and lingering kiss I would have liked, but my best energies had been ignited.

Perfect time to have another run at that poem about how knowing they're not forever can make the lingering embraces sweeter.

Embrace

as I approach the end
never sure the end of what,   certainly of my span
birth - death
it all comes into ever sharper focus
as I see that this impending   I   that
approaches
like a long-ago star   whose fading once-upon-a-time
light
faintly but surely makes its mark on the Hubble
giving a glimpse of what the psalmists were singing
about,
this   I
gracefully redistributing   diffusing the light
so wonderfully organized mere decades ago into

an   I
that danced and swam, rested, wept, worked, wondered,
wished
cheated, fucked, forgot, ate, shat, laughed, tripped,
    hoped,
stank, abandoned and embraced, chewed, choked,
vomited
now winding down   its light dimming
no longer blinding
now the naked eye
can bear its softer, gentler light

odd the focus becoming sharper even as the edges grow
    more fuzzy
blurred   so it can be considered by even the most
fragile eyes

and as it fades it's distinctly
me
or   I
and more like,   well like
can you come up with an image for what causes your
    seemingly sharp boundaries to
blur   smudge
and where there's been anxiety disappointment
admit ecstasy

orgasm?

That's it. Ecstasy

exploding, exceeding, excreting
exiting into universal
embrace

Yes, slower on the trigger without doubt, but happy skin to skin can still trump everything else, at least for the moment. Maybe have an old-age run at that kundalini yoga thing again.

◡

Morning walk with Gabby. I never mastered the meditation thing, but Gabby-walks can turn anxious energy to insight.

This morning Gabby was in major terrier mode, pulling against the leash whenever we came within sniffing range of a bush, or dirt pile from holes the voles dug, or whatever other delights my lackluster nose and eyes don't detect.

"Seems cruel, Gabby, that we keep you under tight control when everything in you wants to chase rodents. I've had my share of leashes: the church, marriage, dishes, grocery shopping. Do you suppose you and I would really like being turned loose? Maggie's giving me a whiff of the freedom I guess I've always had but never saw. Like you, I fantasize about being given my head to chase my primitive energy. Probably you and I would come back looking for the leash before we'd been un-tethered long."

Gabby looked up at me, his head cocked in that beguiling way. Clearly he understood every word. "You know, Gabby,

I don't think I ever imagined becoming this domesticated. But I am. I accuse Alice of trying to make me even more docile. I think she really believes we're both untamable and, you know, Gabby, there's got to be part of her that is happy about that. I'm mostly content, not nearly as restless as I once was. Aging is merciful. Hope it's working like that for you, too."

⌒

"So Maggie, I'm feeling upbeat today. If you've got something up your sleeve you've been sparing me, this might be the moment."

Hearty laugh from Maggie. "You ate your Wheaties, Henry."

I was grateful she didn't tease me about what she no doubt knew of Alice and my night. Sex still embarrasses you, Henry, after a long career listening and guiding people through intimacy issues. What must it be like to be young now, sex having become such common commerce? Plenty of Victorian remnant in you, old boy.

"Yep, a bowlful. No need to go easy on me today."

"Fasten your seatbelt, dear boy."

I saw myself standing in the front hall of the house in Charleston, Ben standing above me. How old was I? Eight? Nine? I had a flashback. Heart thumping.

"Henry," Ben's solemn baritone takes my morning good feeling down a notch. Did he use that voice with Maggie, or my sisters? "I'm going to be away on business for several days and you will be the Papa of this house. It's your responsibility to look after your mother and your sisters until I return."

Sweat trickled down my sides. Sweat from my 60-year-old armpits, or from my eight-year-old armpits? You told Maggie you were up for this. Anxiety is your teacher, Henry, it won't kill you.

"Maggie," I whispered. Was I afraid Ben would hear? "How old am I here?"

Maggie's response was warm, tender. "You're eight, Henry."

"Yes, Daddy, I promise." Queasy stomach, hearing me try to lower my child voice, sound manly. Scene dissolves.

"Maggie, you were there, right? You saw that happen between Ben and me?"

"Yes, Henry, I did."

"Did it happen often?"

"Well, maybe not always with quite so heavy a charge. But every time Ben went away, and he was on the road a lot in those days, he would make a small ceremony of deputizing you to be the authority in his stead."

My head swam.

"Maggie, my God! Did you ever object to Ben's doing that? I mean putting an eight year old in that kind of pressure cooker is gross, not to mention insulting to the other parent—you, Maggie—implying you were incompetent to take charge in his absence."

"The most mind-boggling part, Henry, is how ordinary it was in 1948 for a father to want his eight year old son to consider himself in charge in his stead. It was considered training, preparation for taking charge as a man."

"But come on—why didn't you jump in and let him know how that made *you* feel? Made *me* feel. Was he being literal, or just doing boy-training?"

"Your call. Feelings, Henry? In those days feelings were consigned to movies and novels. And women. It's not that Ben was some monster, torturing you, or me. He didn't think grownups, responsible people *had* feelings. Or at least give them serious consideration when there was work to be done."

"Oh yeah, they do get in the way, don't they?"

"I understand why you'd be angry, Henry, that I didn't challenge your father. If that nice feeling of being intact you came up here with hasn't totally dissolved, and there's enough left of your adult self to take it in, you might consider the angst it can still rouse in you. Whether there is a remnant of it in that dance you and Alice do about who runs the show. There are a lot of moving parts in every family, around power and authority, between genders. The feminist movement hasn't taken them all out of play."

"So, Maggie, how come you put up with Ben when he treated you like his geisha, as if you were simple-minded, incapable of taking care of things? What the hell was with that?"

"I drank. And you, Henry? About the unresolved issues in your long marriage to Alice. All those times she dismisses your hurt feelings or probably is unaware of them? And you keep quiet? Not the same maybe, but I daresay powerfully related.

"Ben was a thoroughly decent man, probably kinder than most husbands those days. He never knowingly hurt me, or you. He was consumed by wanting to do the right thing—desperate for success, frantic that he never got clear in his own mind what success would have looked like. A product of his time. His world had tight borders, defined by the commercial culture to which he gave his best energies. It's important for you to see that he was an honorable man, faithful to his loyalties as best as he could understand them."

The scene in our old front hall had shaken me. It was merciful of Maggie to portray the only father I had with such compassion. She wasn't finished with today's lesson.

"Hard as it is for you to see, Henry, despite your relentless power struggles, Alice is as bound to you as you are to her. Your contentious marriage, such disparate personalities and careers, you fight like characters in a sitcom. You're hardly the first couple to try that, but you're maybe a little unusual in that neither of you has surrendered your strong will to the other. Yet you've worked out how to keep going, leaving considerable room for creativity for each of you. And neither of you has killed the other."

Come pretty close a couple of times.

"Maybe not the calm, easy marriage you fantasized about, but the only kind you two could have made work. And, by Jesus, you have, for over thirty years.

"Why, it's enough to make you believe in the Holy Ghost."

Even I could laugh with her about that.

"Yeah, but you and Ben splitting up after nearly forty

years takes some of the comfort out of our thirty years. Why couldn't the same thing have been true for your marriage? Did the Holy Ghost give up on you two?"

"Yes, Henry, I think she did. It was a different time and we had a different marriage. We were married in 1936. I barely made it through finishing school; never considered college. Ben, terrified the Depression was going to take us down, assumed—so did I until I discovered how ill-suited I was—that I would be a dutiful wife, good mother, always happy to take his lead, never challenge him.

"He'd work himself to the bone, and I'd keep the home fires burning."

My turn to laugh. "That arrangement would have lasted maybe a week with Alice," I said, imagining Alice making beds and dusting the furniture.

"I never learned to play bridge in Charleston nor Mahjong in Manila." Maggie said. "If Ben had been paying attention, that might have clued him in to the trouble that lay ahead."

"And there was your boozing."

"I would have been a boozer even if I'd been a killer lawyer. My father was an alcoholic, pretty much like I was, and he had a thriving medical practice until my mother died. Ben himself was what people your age would now call a functioning alcoholic until he quit drinking; managed to do a creditable enough job to rise to a pretty high level in the company."

"The only thing Ben said, when I asked him one time why he left you, was that he was tired of you getting sauced every night."

"He was, can't blame him. But until he retired, and was around a lot, he hadn't objected to my drinking. We used to both drink pretty heavily every night when he was working. When he retired, he decided to give up drinking. And he did. I admired him for that but never had any interest in quitting myself."

"And that's what broke up your marriage, his going on the wagon and you still drinking?"

"No, what broke up our marriage was his no longer having enough to distract him from his disappointments after he wasn't going to the office every day. As he began to pay attention, he could no longer hang on to the illusions he had about our life and our marriage."

"And you, Maggie? Had you always known it was an illusion?"

"Oh Henry, for all your keen, pastoral insight, you can be obtuse when it suits you. No life, certainly no marriage, can survive without a certain amount of illusion. The issue is how much we acknowledge it without letting it define us. It's why we like movies, understand they aren't reality.

"My mother never finished high school, never had a job, never had a driver's license (though she learned to drive and sometimes did, to our family's horror). She was, to all appearances, pretty, demur, satisfied. That's how she showed herself to the world and, except when pissed, to your grandfather.

"She was a closet subversive, like her parents, like you, Henry, a jujitsu fighter, never openly resisting being dominated, acknowledging, absorbing it, doing a ropa-dope, hanging on the ropes until she chose to make her move. Willingly supporting illusion until she no longer was."

"What do you mean, 'like *me*?'"

"Henry, when you told Ben you were going to seminary, he was crestfallen, and elated, all at once. Crestfallen that you were dropping out of what he saw as the rough-and-tumble life that he believed makes a man a man. And elated that you had found a way to remain, at least peripherally, in the world he considered legitimate. As you knew, he never really understood his father's vocation, but he feared and respected him. That's what saved your bacon with Ben."

"Ha! That's uncomfortably like how I saw it when I told you that I was going to seminary."

"I knew that, Henry. I also was confident you would eventually discover the subversive Zen puzzles the Jesuses and Buddhas sponsored. Alternatives to dominating without surrendering legitimate authority."

Nicely put, Maggie. She was on a roll.

"Marriage isn't the best setting for working that out. But since neither you nor Alice will make peace by yielding, the other, jujitsu, acknowledging, respecting each other's power and learning to absorb and convert it to your own use, is the most creative strategy that doesn't end in divorce or murder.

"Marriage powered by alternative energy. Instead of struggling to deplete the other's power, you absorb it the way solar and wind absorb energy, turn it to your own use."

I'd almost forgotten my burning sciatic. "Brilliant, Maggie! I could have used that great analogy in some of the dead-end marriage counseling I did."

"You won't find this in marriage manuals, Henry. No one under fifty years old, married fewer than twenty-five years, could fathom it, let alone pull it off. But it is the only way people like you and Alice can sustain a long, creative marriage that is neither stand-off nor surrender."

Maggie's description of Alice and my marriage could just as well describe how I tried to make sense of Jesus-power. Can't say I've ever made much sense of either Jesus or marriage, but both lay powerful claim to me. Jujitsu, ropa-dope, may be the best fit. Power's always in play, but never the way the world likes to portray it.

I took my weary psyche down the attic stairs.

⤳

At first light the following morning Gabby and I took a tour on our favorite route, through the cemetery, where I entertained the shiver of death in the morning chill. I often do my day's texting perched on the mound by Minnie and Hollis Stetson's graves. Not only because we lived in what everyone in town considers their house (despite our now having lived there longer than they did), but because I get a stronger cell signal from that spot than from anywhere else in our rural town.

I like to text Alfred, the colleague I was most in synch with for my most dicey years as a parish priest. Dicey because I was still trying to sort out if preaching and wearing a turned around collar was a pose or actually fit me. The issue softened with age. But coming to terms with the inscrutable—God, priest, pastor—was like recurring malaria, sometimes acute, sometimes mercifully mild, sometimes indiscernible. Even occasionally no symptoms at all. But always latent, lurking.

Fact is, Henry, you're still sorting that out. But you did make a sort of separate peace with it. When you decided everyone, not only clergy, is working on her own version of pursuing the inexpressible, you didn't beat yourself up about it as much.

"So, Alfred," I texted, "you still in the chase?"

He hadn't responded to my texts since the shit in his life hit a huge fan. I knew he'd see the message, be glad to see it. Ever since he was defrocked for too much sex with too many women, and being stubbornly unrepentant, Alfred had gone underground. I missed him. We were in neighboring parishes during those stormy years when open marriage, prolific sex, radical politics, racial issues, opposition to Vietnam, coalesced into what we persuaded ourselves was a reprise of the chaotic, first century, Jesus movement.

When I tasted the limits of what even a left of center parish could tolerate, I held my fire. Alfred did the opposite, which made him a sort of Jesus figure to me. It cost him dearly, as he was stripped of all the markings of his office. To Alice, it confirmed that he was foolhardy, self-destructive.

Despite her harsh judgment, like every woman I ever saw around him, Alice loved Alfred. For years she denied it. Until one evening we had a long, alcohol-laden dinner with Alfred, during which she poured her heart out to him, telling him things about her childhood and her well-concealed fears she battled in her law practice she'd never revealed to me. As we were cleaning up later, I teased her about it.

"You don't just *love* him, Alice, you're *besotted*."

"OK, Henry, he's magnetic, a Svengali, but that hardly makes him an admirable priest. He needs to learn to keep it in his pants."

He didn't. I doubt he ever tried. He paid plenty for it. His wife—a thoroughly nice, and very rich, woman who adored him, smothered him with expensive gifts—was outraged when his multiple affairs surfaced. She cut him off, instantly. Totally.

Penniless and stripped of his priestly office, Alfred rejected my pleas that he crawl back to her, abject and penitent. "I'd rather die," he said. So far as I knew he hadn't yet, but he had gone to ground. These infrequent, mostly one-way, one-line texts were our sole remaining connection.

"How're things at the house, Henry?"

Had Gabby not startled, I would have assumed I was hearing my own reverie about Alfred.

"Happy you found that old post in the cellar and rehabbed it to support the porch roof. Always loved the turn on that post, but it didn't work with the Victorian look we gave the place when we wrapped the porch all the way round the house in 1931."

Gabby whined. I felt weary. Enough already. The house is fine, so long as we don't mind paying four thousand dollars for oil to keep from freezing to death in winter. We were thrilled to find that old post, thank you. Yes, everyone still calls it the Stetson House, usually just Minnie Stetson's house. Probably call it Alice Simpson's house after I'm dead.

So that's why you chose this grave lot on this rise, Minnie, where you can keep an eye on the house. Last Christmas Alice and I gave each other plots in the row on that slope, where we intend to haunt our heirs. Not to be rude, Minnie, but I don't plan on having a conversation with you. Nothing personal. I love living in your house. I admire your pink marble Vermont gravestone. But the conversation with Maggie in the attic—I've got scars on my scalp from those roofing nails you never finished off —is all the spooky exchanges I'm good for.

I was sure I felt the ground tremble. Gabby gave a mighty yank on the leash, all ten pounds of him, nearly pulling me over. The sun peeked over the hill, drying the morning dew.

"Come on, Gabby, let's get going. Who's to say every corpse in this graveyard isn't going to take advantage of the one stiff in town willing to talk to them?" I didn't have to ask him twice. We made it home in record time, and when we came into the kitchen, Gabby made straight for his water bowl, noisily slurping for an unusually long time, as if we'd crossed a desert.

Whatever to make of Maggie—Minnie Stetson—will be made clear soon enough. No hurry.

Time to unwind that poem that's been keeping me awake. My editor's getting sick of my adding new ones, pushing back the publication date, but she'll be OK when she sees this one. After all, it's about fear…

Who's Afraid of the Big Bad...?

Fear can cause a curious
commotion.
provoking certain symptoms we recognize
nausea
headache, sweaty palms and arm
pits,
it doesn't have its own well-defined, clearly recognized
character.
Not like pain from a wound or accident, or world
weariness
after hard work or exercise, not like
depression
driven by loss or sickness or the unkind
edge
of reality wedging aside illusion.

More like an inner
ear
infection disturbing balance, blurred or tunnel
vision
suggesting the need for new eye
glasses.

Fear that clings, doesn't
dissipate
when the danger does

the near collision, the stock
market's dizzying descent,
doctor's lingering look at that
mole,
her furrowed brow as she returns the stethoscope to the same
    spot the
third time;
Long breath, now let it out slowly...

When the fear lingers, begins to
gnaw
then rouse
anger
the body signals its
desire
to ... to? Sleep, flee, defecate, die, lash out, placate, hide, con-
    front,
go to the movies?
Whatever will shift the mix, for the moment,
geld the
beast.

Chronic fear, is, I think,
peculiar
to our kind. Our evolutionary kin can call up
adrenaline
in an instant, and when he doesn't die,
release it.
do Impala suffer
headache, nervous nausea, heart

burn?
does chronic fatigue make a monkey
impotent?

Perhaps there is some as yet
undiscovered
gain for us in this relentless
anguish.
But I suspect Gautama got it right
unsettling though it is
we choose this
as our hedge against
abyss,
refusing reassurance
that reality is ample,
ego's pointless pursuit of personal
perfection,
forever
fueling fear.

You know what, Gabby, Maggie's right; I'm a decent poet, better than I'll usually admit. OK, Alice, and most of my parishioners, don't get it. So? Like *I* do? Some of the best pieces of me emerge from that place that floats in the viscous sea of the unconscious where the mysteries mostly remain submerged. High time they got some air.

Buoyed by finishing work I'd been putting off, I was ready to greet Alice without being defensive about whether she'd consider my day well spent. Gabby was back at me, his infallible clock, barking for his supper. Could a whole day have gone by since our morning walk? What must it be like to sleep, untroubled, all day, your stomach rousing you twice, excitement peaking as friskies are poured into your dish, snarf them down in thirty seconds, then return to dormant, untroubled calm?

"Could be worse ways to spend a day, huh Gabby?"

Out for walk number three. Gabby, fed, rested, perky. Nice evening. Sun dropping behind the mountain, twilight through the maples. Breeze died, the quiet broken by the crow on that high branch, complaining to the barn swallows that scold and low-fly him.

⤳

Alice's car was in the driveway when we arrived home. As we entered the house I picked up the towel in the hallway and wiped the dirt from Gabby's paws before letting him race in to find Alice. She was in the den at the far end of the hall. Her voice lacked its usual enthusiasm as she greeted Gabby. Uh oh, must have had a wearying day. Maybe I could cajole her.

"Hi Alice, how nice to have you home early."

"Hello, Henry."

Uh oh, downer voice. "Tough day?"

"Not particularly."

Iceberg voice.

"What's up?"

"I've been reading your journal."

Oh shit! "Journal? I don't keep one any more."

"This is one from a few years ago. I found it on the floor at the foot of the attic stairs."

Shit, shit, shit! I bet I dropped the thing when I was carrying that stuff to the garage. God knows what she read.

"Oh?" I walked down the hall to the den where Alice was sitting at her desk. My old journal, open on the desk in front of her. She didn't look up at me.

"I had no idea that's the way you feel about me, Henry. I've never been so devastated. It's hateful."

"What way, Alice?" Shit, shit, shit! What's *in* that journal?

"That your whole life is about humoring me, trying to keep me from acting like the nasty bitch you think I am most of the time. That you dream of having sex with those women who fawn over you. Have you any idea how hurtful that is, Henry? It's disgusting to discover the truth about what my husband of over thirty years really thinks about me."

She was whining. I rarely heard that from tough, lawyer Alice. The last time was when our daughter Madelyn told Alice she thought she was a cruel, unloving mother. Her whine made me so anxious I had an extra heartbeat.

"Alice, what's the date on that journal?" Goddamn it, how could I be so careless?

"I don't care what date it is, Henry, it's *your* journal, where you wrote your real feelings. The things you never dared say out loud to me."

"You've got it totally wrong, Alice. That's from twelve years ago, when life between us was night-and-day different from how it is now. My journal then was my psychotherapist, where I let fly whatever came to me, no filter, so I could look at it and reconsider it, reshape how I wanted my life to be. I never worried about someone else reading it because I wrote it only for myself. Had I ever imagined anyone else would read it—certainly you—I would never have been so unguarded. I considered my journal confidential, needing no censor, like talking to a shrink."

Alice began to cry. I curbed my impulse to try to comfort her. She spoke haltingly through her sobs: "Well, now that I *have* read it, nothing can ever erase those hurtful things you wrote. Now that I know what you really think, I don't see how I could be expected to go on living with someone who secretly hates me. What other terrible secrets have you been keeping from me, Henry? How many other women have you turned to—probably fucked—because you hated me, didn't find me attractive? Or nice?"

I shivered. "Secrets is exactly what those are," I said, hearing the bitterness in my own voice, "and they were meant to be *kept* secret, Alice! If people knew each other's secret thoughts there would be no friendships, and there sure as hell wouldn't be any marriages that lasted beyond the honeymoon. It's the same as if I could read your thoughts." God help us all. "If I could, I'm sure I'd be just as hurt and devastated as you are right now by nasty things you think about me. Out of kindness and wisdom, you keep them to yourself, until those destructive thoughts are overruled by saner ones. Everyone, and sure as hell every marriage, needs places where it's safe to have private, unacceptable, potentially destructive thoughts. Until this moment I had always considered my journal one of those places."

Her crying grew louder, her breath coming in choking

gasps. "You're just trying to use your bullshit, psycho-bab-
ble, fucking, no-conscience, pastor crap, to wiggle out of it,
Henry, you heartless bastard!"

Gloves-off time. "Fucking right, I'm trying to get out of it,
Alice! Because if I can't—if you won't admit that you could
just as easily have written something just like this, about me,
then we may as well hang up on our marriage. It's not like
I'm hiding some big secret, or that I secretly hate you, the
way you imagine right now. Like everyone, I have moments
when I don't like *anyone*, not our kids, not you, not Gabby,
not my own self. Not fucking God. And if those thoughts are
outlawed, or have to be put up for public inspection, then
there is no way we—or anyone—could hope to live under
the same roof for long."

Alice quieted a little, her crying calmed to a whimper.

Did she actually hear me?

"But, Henry, how can you possibly live with someone
once you know they have all those terrible feelings about
you? How can you ever look each other in the eye again
without thinking about all that nasty shit?"

"Well, Alice, that's the sixty-four thousand dollar question, isn't it?" How come I feel so calm all of a sudden?
"Most of the time we forget about the second half of that
for-better-for-worse marriage vow. You know the biggest reason marriages break up? When the for-worse part
comes, they feel cheated, screwed, like they hadn't signed
on for that part. God knows, you and I have had plenty
of times when no one would have blamed us, or been surprised, if we had split up. So how come we didn't, Alice?
Sure as hell not because we are two such noble people,

or the types who are particularly good at overlooking the nasty shit we sometimes do, or say, or think, about each other."

I paused for a breath, maybe I'd said enough. Quiet, Henry, wait for Alice. The two of us stood, awkwardly, half-facing each other, trying vainly to rearrange our facial expressions into something more mature, less adolescent and petulant, wishing we could feel more grownup. Alice broke the silence.

"And why do *you* think that is, Henry, that we have hung in all these years?" Her tone dripped with sarcasm. "Because we *adore* each other so much we never even *think* any of those hurtful things?"

I guffawed. Alice struggled to hang onto her angry face, then lost it, echoing my guffaw. We stood a foot apart, our bodies shaking with laughter.

Alice choked, gasping, between laughter and tears. I regained myself enough to speak. "That must be it, Alice. How else can you explain these touching, movie-worthy, romantic moments so common with us that everyone must think they define our marriage?"

"Now that's cruel, Henry, a low blow. Maybe we aren't your lovey-dovey couple; I like to think we're more willing to face reality than so many couples pretending to live some Walt Disney fantasy."

Now that felt hugely welcome. "Sorry, Alice, I hadn't meant to sound cruel. I actually believe it *is* our love for each other that has kept us together, even though we're masters at pushing each other's hot buttons. Or maybe we can so quickly hit each other's hot buttons precisely because we love each other and know each other's insides.

And because, as you said, we don't detour around the hard realities."

"Honestly, Henry?" Alice's voice was calm. "Do you really believe our conflict is driven by our love for each other?"

"I do, Alice. It's our fucked-up culture, not the two of us, that translates love into sappy, bullshit emotion. Love, or whatever makes people stay together, isn't just some adolescent heart-flip. It's a disciplined, demanding, mature act of will. The Elizabethans, who wrote those marriage vows in the Prayer Book, were screwed up about a lot of things, but they didn't think uninterrupted, sweet, cheery feelings was what makes a marriage last."

"So then, what *does*, wise, Reverend, Father Henry?"

Ignore that sarcasm, Henry. "You're the smartest, toughest, lawyer I know, Alice; you write and enforce contracts. Marriage is a contract. What makes a contract work?" Easy does it here, Henry.

"Is that a serious question, Henry, or just a point for you to win the argument?"

"Deadly serious."

"Well, I'd say what makes a contract work is tedious research into every imaginable eventuality that one could conceive; exhaustive searching for anything that could negatively impact the agreement. The purpose of a contract is to head off that inevitable moment when the good intentions it began with, turn sour. Circumstances change. So you write in language making it an obligation, binding the parties to the contract, even in the face of eventualities that could cause them to want the contract to become null and void."

I waited for a moment before saying, "You mean eventualities like, for better, for worse, in sickness and in health, 'til death us do part?"

I hadn't noticed Gabby leave his cushion and come over to where Alice and I were still standing toe to toe. He whimpered, as he does when our voices rise in anger. He scratched Alice's leg, which I translate as, "Everything's going to be all right, isn't it?" Raised voices make a terrier (and you, Henry) anxious. No wonder couples are reluctant to let out the clutch on their anger.

Like the good lawyer she is, Alice paused before responding. Like a good lawyer, she answered my question with one of her own.

"And if they do really loathsome, unforgivable things that make them hate each other so much they don't care what they've signed? Some contracts do become unenforceable, you know Henry."

"Alice, have you ever written a contract that became unenforceable because something happened to piss off one of the parties? Or if—no, when—the moment comes when they hate each other, no longer want to keep to the terms of what they've signed?"

Alice laughed again. "So who's the freaking attorney here? Are you describing how you're feeling right now?"

"Alice, do you think I'd be working this hard if I wanted out? I'd like to add one more clause to our marriage contract, Alice—that each party is forbidden to read the other's private journals."

"Well, that's going to require a sub-clause nullifying that clause if you're asshole enough to drop yours in the hallway where I'm going to trip over it."

"Don't you worry your pretty little head about that, my sweet. Not only will I see to burning any old journals I may unearth, but I was done a long time ago with keeping one. Too much temptation to write in them whenever I'm feeling picked on by you and sorry for myself. And too much temptation for you to read them—no matter what's in the contract."

"And as you know perfectly well, Henry, I've never kept a journal; always thought they were a stupid, self-indulgent, narcissistic waste of time."

"Right, Alice, you've kept your spiteful feelings about me safely hidden in your head. Except for when I forget to puff up the pillows and maybe when you're out with a few of your girlfriends and have the extra glass of wine."

Crazy to get into defending my journal-keeping, just when it looks like we may yet get through this without blood-letting.

"Alice, we've been standing here for twenty minutes; how about we call a truce? Why don't you go change your clothes while I finish getting dinner ready. And by the way, we may need to resurrect that old trash barrel in the corner of the garage to fit all the stuff I brought down from the attic today to throw away. Including—you ready for this?—every one of my exam blue books from seminary."

"Oh Henry!" Alice wrapped her arms around me as I stood, awkwardly, her embrace making me unable to return her hug. "I do make your life miserable, don't I? I really don't mean to be such an insufferable asshole."

I wriggled free so I could return her embrace. "Oh Allie, we're a perfectly matched set of insufferable assholes. You've got nothing to apologize for. I make my own life miserable when I'm not making yours miserable. That nasty stuff you read truly isn't how I feel about you in my sane moments. It's just what everyone and everything in the whole world can look like to me when I've sunk into one of my patented despairs."

"You can't imagine how much I want to believe that, Henry. Alice clutched me closer, her tears coming again."

"No more than I want you to, Allie."

I picked up the journal from her desk, carried it into the living room, leaned down, stuffed it between the logs I had earlier laid in the fireplace. I lit a match to the paper under the grate, The flames caught the kindling and, quickly, the journal. "Look, Allie, it's burning with a deep green flame."

"You really don't have to do that for me, Henry. Burning it doesn't have anything to do with whether I think you really meant all those hateful things."

"I'm burning it for *me*, Alice, more than for you. It's from a time, now, thank God, long ago, when I was trying to make you wear the shit that belongs to me. The last thing I need is to keep a journal, or anything else, that makes it easier for me to nurse my secret wounds instead of tending to them like a sensible person."

"Jesus, Henry, every now and then you sound frighteningly like a grownup. I hope you never expect such mature behavior from me." Her laughter finally trumped her tears.

I laughed too. "I don't honestly know what I expect from you, Alice, except that I hope like hell you'll stick around while we keep growing up into whatever it is we signed on for more than thirty years ago."

"Contract still very much in force, Henry, and this party to it is way more grateful for that than she ever lets on."

I took three steps from the fireplace to where Alice stood by the living room door. Side by side we watched the flames consume the journal, the green color receding until the first log was fully engaged, bright orange. I turned toward Alice, embracing her. She shifted, leaning into me, our bodies touching, knees to chests, warming each other.

"Sealed with…" I said, kissing her with my lips soft, parting. She responded with her warm, welcome tongue.

That night in bed, we each put our books on our bedside tables and turned off our reading lights at the same time, not the usual reading ourselves to sleep. Alice rolled onto her side toward me.

"Thank you, Henry, I know that was as hard for you as it was for me."

"I've been through that same issue with so many couples in counseling, but it's totally different when it's us. I hated that you read that, but it seems like it took us someplace we needed to go."

She stayed on my side of the bed, very still.

"I'm still kind of worried about something, Henry."

Jesus, what now? "What?"

"That if you don't write all those terrible things about me in your journal—things I wish weren't, but I know are true—you're going to end up running up a huge shrink bill that will bankrupt us."

Laughter from us both. "Well, Sweetheart, that's nothing a fat lawyer's salary and wholesale sex can't take care of."

The big income was a slam dunk, and Alice generously showed her enthusiasm for contributing to the other side of that prescription as well.

～

For the next several days, as I digested that encounter with Alice, I took a timeout from Maggie and cleared out almost everything left in that old box, careful to keep my hands off Maggie's book. I worked on the poem I intended for the centerpiece of the book nearing publication. It's a good poem, just needs something to make it pop. Pop, Henry? Are you a marketing manager or a poet? Shameless huckster or serious writer? Familiar quarrel with myself. I knew the answer: both.

Once I got the thing working the way I hoped, I showed it to my editor. She pronounced it ready for prime time.

Three Score and Then Some

Sometime
a decade or so ago I
noticed I wasn't so strong or
supple
as I once was. I have no
idea
whether something special woke my
awareness

or was it gentle, gradual and one day I saw it?

I once believed I'd be smarter when my body
began
to check out
you know, compensation, but I don't think
so any more.
Wiser? Maybe, if you believe there is
such a thing as wiser,
not just another of our brainchildren to soften the
blow
as we're sliding
losing our foothold on the
Darwinian edge
we once thought we'd firmly grasped for
good.

I reckoned how old I was when my
dad
was my age.
33. thought I'd slipped over the edge by
then. I was straddling more than one chasm,
hating the Vietnam
war   while
pastor of a parish filled with super
patriots who hated my long curly
hair and bell bottoms maybe more than my politics.
At least that's the excuse I used for why they froze
me out of

their clubs.

Walter Reed was on my beat
for a while.
I got to know one guy, about my
age
who'd taken a 30 caliber round in the
forehead
and lived
sort of, they'd screw another metal plate to his
skull
until the bone frizzled and they'd do it again but
they were running out of skull, getting close to his
brain.
He'd sit on the big Walter Reed lawn of an afternoon
in conversation with the guy
who had no
arms or
legs
They kept telling him how lucky he was to have been in
    Nam where the choppers got
you out in minutes.

My office looked over
Lafayette Park across the street from the
White House.
I could see into the park from my
second story perch over the fence that
President Nixon

had built to keep out the protesters, the fence covered with
    anti-war
graffiti.
At a demonstration one morning a lovely long-haired
lady said to me, "If Nixon had to come out in the
morning and sit astride a bucket in Lafayette Park and do
    his
business
the war would be over that day." Set me thinking about the
    guy with no arms
or legs
the waste product The President was privileged to elimi-
    nate
in private.

I'm well past
mid life now
grousing
with old friends
about how they changed all the
rules
while we were in mid
stream until
our revolution swallowed its tail and vomited out
us.

The 60s, they now say, was about
sex
about the Victorian rules finally losing their
grip

on us. But I'd say it was about what every age is about
desperation
the aweful discovery that no one is in
charge
and no one knows how things will come
out
and perhaps Freud, discredited as he is, was right about
God
and how we invent God and project onto
(H)im
what we wish and can't win for ourselves.

We did
therapy
and then
divorced
and had our adolescent thrills in our 30s. We thought it
    right that
our kids would be more like the rest of the
world
what with double-digit inflation and flat
wages and Arab oil
would live less like royalty than we
had.
We didn't yet know about
Ronald Reagan and
Hollywood neo-conservatism, the religious
Right nor
Gorbachev and the
evil empire gone belly

up leaving the stars and
stripes the only game in town, free to plunder the
world
and in the holy name of free
enterprise fashion our kids into zillion
aires.

Sometime a decade or less ago
I
discovered that whether Ron or George, his son W, or even
    our sexy 60s
soul mate
Bill
holds the frenzied focus
things unfold and cells keep
aging
their borders blurring, nucleus softening
beguiling boundaries believed
to mark us off not only from the lesser
hemisphere but from
simpler soulless species
who walk this Way—we believed at our peril –
with our forbearance.

Perhaps it's so the
Center
cannot hold
or perhaps it's that the
Center

shifts as cells mutate and once neglected
ganglia gain new purpose as our sweet sister
Death
rolls her tongue around our inner
ear, coos her
siren song enticing us to
turn
into her embrace
finishing soul's longing,
waiving willful work in favor of effortless
ecstasy.

Where does this wild shit come from, Henry? If you can
believe Maggie, it was always there, waiting impatiently.
Depicting the time when domination would no longer be
the measure of worth, potent expression of your confidence that Maggie and Julian of Norwich are right: all will
be well, and all manner of things shall be well.

⌒

The near disaster of Alice reading my journal set me to
wondering about how our family had managed secrets. I
had my own; Maggie didn't lack for her share. What did
we do with them in my family growing up? Victoria and
Jean, with more marriages than I, harbored many secrets
I knew about, some I'm sure I didn't, with the potential to
blow families apart.

An email exchange with Victoria and Jean proved fertile.

Emails:

From: Henry
To: Victoria
cc: Jean

Recently I had this exchange with Alice that led to near blood-letting (no need for details). It resolved by our allowing as to how some secret, not-so-nice thoughts about each other are inevitable, and usually better left secret. Need not wreck your marriage. Led me to wondering about Maggie, and our great grandmothers, Sylvia in Cuba, Sarah in Florida. Each maintained the outward appearance of docile, conventional, maybe even passionless women, subservient to their husbands. Maggie, now you two, have helped me see they wielded a hell of a lot of power. In practical ways, maybe more than their husbands. Someone looking on from the outside could easily think they lived their whole lives in their husbands' shadows. Turns out, though subtle, they used their power to make a lot happen. This was a surprise to me. Was it to you?

From: Jean
To: Henry
cc: Victoria

No. I bought Mom's (sorry I still can't do the Maggie thing) façade as a kid, but when I was about sixteen, I saw Dad's I'm-in-charge persona was mostly posturing. Maggie and us kids let it stand to make life run smoothly. Go along to get along. He was the noisiest, eager to be in charge. How did I come to see through his pose? Sixteen was when I had my first serious boyfriend. I read him like a not-very-complicated book, a life-changing revelation after years of being intimidated by Dad's bluster. I wondered, even at that young age, what's with you guys, needing to look so in-charge, when I was pretty sure you don't have any better handle on what's going on than we do? Is that supposed to impress us?

From: Victoria
To: Jean
cc: Henry

Ha, ha, Jean. That I'm-in-charge, guy-thing was just another clumsy attempt to get in your pants.

From: Henry
To: Victoria
cc: Jean

I feel retarded about all this compared to you two. Was I the only one in our family left in the dark? And how about giving us guys a break; sex is no more than 99% of what we were after. We also hope for an occasional good meal.

From: Victoria
To: Henry
cc: Jean

Ha, ha, Henry, well said. No, you weren't the only one.

Dad (or Ben, as you prefer) was in the dark, too. And maybe Birdie, the beagle.

From: Jean
To: Victoria
cc: Henry

Ha, ha! We worried that Birdie might have started to see the light and reveal our secret cabal to overturn Dad's rule. That's why we had that car run over Birdie.

From: Henry
To: Jean
cc: Victoria

Now, that's cruel, Jean. You were just as attached as I was to that sweet little beagle.

From: Jean
To: Henry
cc: Victoria

Oh right; so sorry Henry. I almost forgot that it was Jesus who arranged for that car to run over Birdie that afternoon so Mr. Vest would come and comfort you and you would decide to go into the ministry. God works in mysterious ways, huh Henry?

From: Henry
To: Jean

cc: Victoria

OK, OK, you've made your point. This stuff I'm learning from Maggie wasn't the mystery to you two that it was to me. How about all the anti-establishment, revolutionary stuff in our family history? Were you in on that, too?

From: Victoria
To: Henry
cc: Jean

No, I wasn't. But then I've never been as interested in politics as you are. In fact, I take most of my clues about all that from you.

You're a remarkable man, Henry; I'm proud to be your sister. I've known few men (hell, damn few women, for that matter) willing, this late in life, to reconsider so many things they'd set in concrete. But you are still a guy. Most guys learn about revolution, politics, gender—especially gender, intimacy—from comics and movies. And from bullies. You reinforce those caricatures, bragging and lying to each other. Am I surprised that you're discovering the women in our family wielded more power in the family than was apparent? Maybe even had a hand in revolution? Only in the details. Since I am one, I do know something about the women in our family. And even though I was sad—and pissed—to see Mom turn to booze, become a recluse, I knew her dysfunction hid strengths you're seeing in her now. She was one of us, same gene pool as Jean and me, and, even though from a different gene pool, your feisty wife. Guess we're pretty challenging to guys who think they ought to be in charge.

From: Jean
To: Victoria
cc: Henry

And—for those men who can handle it—the coolest women any man could hope to hook up with.

From: Henry
To: Victoria
cc: Jean

So where the fuck was I when you two were soaking up all this wisdom?

From: Jean
To: Henry
cc: Victoria

Don't take this wrong, Henry, but you were Dad's son, only son, no brothers to bounce it off. You tracked him like a disciple, the model you thought you were supposed to become. He was a good enough man, decent father, good provider, and a pretty able businessman. But when it came to real power versus sham power, well, he either couldn't see it or didn't want it to distract him from selling soap and making his way up the corporate ladder. I thought he woke up a little before he died, but even then it was as if he was following someone else's script, never wrote one for himself.

From: Victoria
To: Henry
cc: Jean

You do know, I hope, Henry, that script Dad followed when he changed course near the end of his life was the script you wrote for him. Who would have imagined Ben becoming a civil rights guy or anti-war? He even tried out a little corporate bashing after, of course, leaving P&G. You may have felt you never lived up to whatever he wanted, but before he died, he tried to live up to what he thought you wanted from him.

From: Henry
To: Jean
cc: Victoria

Oh God, you two, I've been living in a Dagwood and Blondie comic strip. I get weary of the guy-bashing that's a staple of the women's movement, American literature and movies. I get how the macho agenda, in an anxiety-ridden, pseudo-patriarchal culture, blocks out authentic male psyche. But there were lots of us who chose a different path, weren't totally seduced by mindless success and faux domination. Sometimes it seems women care more about taking revenge for men's posturing and bullying than making things work for both genders.

FYI. I didn't miss what you said about Ben reading from my script before he died. I was aware of that, but you can't imagine how weird it seemed.

From: Victoria
To: Henry
cc: Jean

No need to defend yourself, or your gender, to us, Henry. You're too hard on yourself. Do you expect to be totally evolved? Your church career looked pretty authentic to me, more than you were willing to claim for yourself.

Dr. King, The Fellowship of Reconciliation, non-violence, anti-Vietnam War, environment, climate change—all that was about the shifting of power—domination to cooperation. You embraced it; you've actually taken a shot at *living* it. That was risky in those parishes; the money still in the hands of the old boys.

It's a guy-thing, being suspicious of your own motives. You know motives are always mixed. You've been honest about that in yourself. More emotionally available than many of your colleagues. Maybe old Ben inadvertently helped you see how often men's posturing is bullshit.

Your job gave you access to the old power; you could have chosen to opt in. You just looked silly in three piece suits.

Glad Maggie's helping you make peace with that. Your unwillingness, or maybe you were clueless, to do that male power thing, must have made you feel like you were always in deficit. But it's one reason women, like your sisters and your wife, are drawn to you. Your affection, and respect, for all sorts of people is transparent. Maybe a little over the top sometimes with women. Good thing you learned a little discretion, and Alice put the skids to you, before you blew up your marriage and your career.

From: Henry
To: Victoria
cc: Jean

Sometimes all I see is the deep shit I got into because I wasn't more savvy about power, especially how women do it. The men power brokers in my parishes thought I had too feminine an agenda. And they weren't crazy about their wives hanging out with me. I kept thinking their wives loved me. And I *do* love being loved.

From: Jean
To: Henry
cc: Victoria

They *did* love you, Henry. Because you are so loveable. The old two-edged sword. They loved you because you're loveable, and for all the fucked up reasons that got you into the deep shit Victoria mentioned in her email.

From: Henry
To: Jean
cc: Victoria

Such as?

From: Jean
to: Henry
cc: Victoria

Don't bother me with the games you played to extricate yourself. Maggie doesn't buy it, and neither do I. Lucky for you, Alice considered it grounds for justifiable homicide.

You know what I'm talking about. That pure, holy, sent-by-Jesus purity. Women telling you how different you were from their money-grubbing, power-hungry, clueless, dismissive husbands, at whom they were always pissed. You could be their savior. And their lover. It's a wonder one of those husbands, after his wife told him one more time what an understanding man you were, didn't assassinate you. Letting yourself be seduced by that bullshit was pretty nearly your undoing. And I don't care how much our fucked-up family left you clueless. You're a savvy guy, Henry. You knew.

From: Victoria
To: Henry
cc: Jean

Not to pile on here, Henry, but being horny and pretending to be clueless about power is a lethal combination.

From: Henry
To: Victoria
cc: Jean

Being oblivious to the way people use power still gives me the willies. Maggie, and you two, getting a look at our ancestors, has brought me face to face with stuff I never screwed up the courage to deal with in therapy.

Did I believe the Gandhi thing about myself? No. Did I dissuade anyone else from believing it? No.

Christ, what a manipulator.

From: Jean
To: Henry
cc: Victoria

Heavy stuff, Henry. So, your motives aren't pure, which makes you like every other authority figure in the western world, male or female, including Gandhi when he put his body in the way of The British Empire. The Margaret Thatchers and Hilary Clintons didn't bother trying to make a case for a different, feminine power, because they'd have been quickly dismissed.

It's true the weirdness of the church made it easier, Henry, but you *did* choose a different kind of power. If we don't extinct ourselves first, it's that power that will shape the world. You should be proud to be in the vanguard.

From: Henry
To: Jean
cc: Victoria

What great sisters!

I'm maxed out. I haven't spoken with Maggie the past couple of weeks. I'll miss it when it's over, and I sense we're nearing the end.

Maggie, and you two, are helping unpack my gender confusion. I'm grateful. Oddly, it makes me want to reclaim my legitimate maleness. This hanging around with all you dames makes me lopsided. In suburban parishes, where women ruled by day, and their husbands commuted, we men clergy talked about that a lot.

One guy at a clergy meeting said, "If I have to go to one more women's meeting this month I'm afraid I may start to menstruate."

Though male menopause has been mostly a blessing for me, I'm not dead yet, my wise, compassionate sisters. Strong feminine side, maybe, but still a guy.

From: Victoria
To: Henry
cc: Jean

Your rock, Henry! I think I still have a few maxi-pads in my medicine cabinet just in case…

From: Henry
To: Victoria
cc: Jean

Though I wish I didn't Victoria, I have my own stash of old-folks' pads in my medicine cabinet, too. Another in the long list of things I never imagined when I was younger.

From: Jean
To: Henry
cc: Victoria

Before we sign off, Henry, I hope you know that Victoria and I think you're the greatest.

Being a principled agnostic has made you a fine priest and pastor. Churches full of anxious, reticent, rich Republicans chose you in spite of your being a thinly disguised, liberal, trouble-making, Democrat. In part *because* you were the closest they could tolerate to a '60s, free-love, hippie. Frightened by their children—and often each other—they sensed something important and irreversible was underway. You were a semi-legitimate, transition figure, dropping clues for how to survive, if not embrace it. Naturally, they wanted to keep you on a short leash.

Your awesome wife, Alice, maybe a fundamentalist about Rules of Evidence and intolerant of your fuzzy boundaries, still, after thirty crazy years, your biggest booster.

You were just damn lucky, Henry.

But somehow, without a lot of posturing, you opened doors for people into places they'd never imagined going.

That Zen thing—trust the process—draws people to you. Makes them believe you. That and your authentic fascination and love for, as the Prayer Book puts it, all sorts and conditions of people.

So, bravo, my Bro!

From: Henry
To: Jean
cc: Victoria

OMG. Overwhelmed! Thanks!

From: Victoria
To: Henry
cc: Jean

Just to keep the record straight, Henry, I'm totally on the same page as Jean about all this, but despite your uncanny resemblance to Jesus and the Mahatma, you'll forever be my beloved, asshole, little bro.

Over and out, dear siblings.

⌐

Poetry began rolling out, a sign of being at home with myself. And, maybe, that my time with Maggie was nearing its finish. Love it when poetry (blank verse actually; I've pissed off many a purist by calling what I write, poetry) flows like water, tuning loose language I hardly recognize as coming from me. My restless editor, also formed by the formless '60s, cheers me on.

Evolutionary Enigma was inspired by my colleague, the local Rabbi's discovery that the cancer he thought would kill him had responded to his stem cell transplant, erasing the plague altogether. The experience turned Marty Levin's life over to the explorer and pleasure-seeker he'd kept in the closet while he served his congregation.

After a long talk with Marty, and seeing the affecting movie, *Crouching Tiger, Hidden Dragon*, this poem seemed to pop onto my computer screen.

Evolutionary Enigma

If you're under 50, you may wish to watch this
over my shoulder,
as
it's about the experiment
beyond
genetic striving,
a recent evolutionary enigma.

This morning I woke in a pool of
euphoria
and spent the day parsing its pieces
Crouching Tiger,   Hidden Dragon,
Mary Oliver's poetry
Marty Levin's long life

Victoria's shoulds   and
classmates' minor memories   morphed
into unexpected ecstasy.

Crouching Tiger tendered freedom from gravity's
weight   for   enchanting
people   bounding   over   roof
                    tops
          skipping cross water like a dragonfly
     never breaking surface tension, rising, soaring
     like Mary Oliver's verse, risking routes too

                    remote

               to chart,   like
          cells that outlive DNA's demands.

My friend Marty the raucous Rabbi, steadfast through
thick
     and thin
     especially thin when lymphoma
     stalked him like the luminary he
     is.   And these years
     later, his cancer quiet, life lately sweet
     Marty gulps each instant whole, famished for what he
always
     craved   and still can't quite
     taste. I'm leaving the pulpit, he told me, his eyes bright as
     stars, and I want to talk to you about how you choose
when

each morning you wake is
yours. Marty and I were ravishing Crown Books'
going-out-of-business Sale
His market basket bore 45 lbs of books. I'm dying, he
said, of curiosity since
    cancer couldn't kill me. I'm ready to be reborn, and

            solo

he uttered irrationally   exuberant.

My sister Victoria says since 60 she hasn't any longer
time
    for obligation's oughts because her
    heart's desires deserve her
    prize energy. And she gives it to them.

Classmates from
forty
years before in late life e-conversation confess clandes-
tine in-
    discretions
    that could have done them
    in, and now are more memorably etched than
    prizes or honors. What we feared if found would
    ruin us
    has become best, bridging
    distance
    enticing us into intimacy we never knew we lacked or
    wanted.

Lest this 60s sentiment seduce
you,
we who unwittingly encounter these
odd events form an
evolutionary enigma,   anomalies
graybeards beyond the bounds of
genetic gain.
And because biological experiments almost always
abort, why not
defy   gravity
flip off the free market
test Grace?

We're warned we'll break the social security/medicare
bank. Perhaps
but more likely,
our scattered cells will watch the way
we exploded orthodoxy
precariously perched on the precipice of
existence
when we passed from purpose into
fancy.

What, after all, have we to lose? After a long
life a little last
gasp
we never
bargained for
bursting with God-only-knows

what
pregnant possibility.

We can't go wrong, not now. We've
burst the boundaries
we once assumed defined the canopy.
We rode the tiger striped with fears and
phobia
that turned, if not tame, at least to terror
we learned to live and
die with.

Alice is right. My poetry's not for everyone. Makes my heart beat faster to let it rip. Maggie, and Marty, helped turn loose much of what had stuck in my ecclesiastical craw all those years. Some parishioners laugh when I suggest I'd kept this stuff under wraps. Guess the wrap didn't look as tight to them as I thought.

So grateful to Maggie, my surprise soundboard, the awesome mother I somehow missed when I was forming up.

One more matter I hoped Maggie might lend a hand with. Nearly down to the bottom of the box, fulfilling my promise to Alice to throw everything, including the rotting box itself, into the trash before her spy case settled or went to trial.

One last secret, hunch?, I'd long entertained.

Cool morning, the attic drier than usual. I opened the book, again to D. All the heavy stuff seemed lodged in the Ds.

"W.E. Damon? Another name in your book that stirred a lot of old juices in me."

I had snacked on some crackers and cheese. My mouth was dry, my tongue sticking to the roof of my mouth. Wish I'd brought some water.

"Blackie Damon is another name that got my juices going. He's not just another name in the book, is he?"

Pause. "In what way, Dear Boy?"

"Well, like he packed more clout with us than a casual family friend. Coming across his name lit up something in me. Not exactly the same, but like the way Andrew Vest's name did.

"I always wondered how he got that nickname, Blackie."

Maggie's laugh. "That was Charleston in the 1940s; you remember what he looked like?"

"I do. Loved his looks. Swarthy, earthy. Raspy voice. Seemed less WASPY than your other friends."

"You got him, Henry. Anything else about him that makes him memorable for you?"

"Well, for one, he was way more available emotionally than most of your men friends, certainly the most approach-able professional man I knew. He treated kids like me as if we counted. Thinking about him now, I wonder—he seemed almost like he could have had a smattering of African in him—which would for sure put him in a different category from your other friends.

"But I suppose that was just his looks, right? I mean he was married to the most delicate, pale-skinned, aristocratic, southern woman I can remember in that bastion of the old Confederacy. And he was a doctor, a surgeon, right? Their over-achieving kids, their aristocratic social lives, everything about the Damons was pure Charleston WASP Except for the warm way he treated me as a kid. And his looks."

Long silence. "Appearances, Henry, how much they conceal. You're right. Charleston, still the old south then, preserving convention at all costs. Keeping up appearances or ignoring appearances that didn't precisely fit. Never coloring outside the lines, if you'll forgive the pun."

One more time, the ground shifting. "So Dr. Damon was one of those we read about with muddy racial identity?" Look at that; I switched from Blackie to Dr. Damon. And how about "muddy"?

"Hardly unique for Charleston in those days. You'd never get any of our friends to so much as hint at such a thing. Blackie was a respected physician, an elder in the Huguenot church, another Charleston peculiar."

"We're talking the deepest fear of the old south—racial mixing, miscegenation." Jesus, Henry, where did that old southern bugaboo come from?

"Blackie Damon's another hero of mine. Pretty special to you, too, right? If medical school hadn't required college chemistry, I might have done that. Because I would have liked to be like him."

"Do you suppose it might have been Blackie's hint of darkness, as well as his kindness, Henry, that attracted you?"

"Another ingredient secretly folded into our DNA—Maggie? Maybe the missing motive for our passion for justice, a vested interest in racial justice?"

"Could be, Henry. You've said you hadn't a noble bone in your body, which made you suspicious of your motives for joining the struggle for racial justice. That it somehow felt more personal than principled, as if you had a stake you could never quite identify."

The big missing piece I came up here hoping to find today.

"Seems like people I grew up with in Charleston ended up clearly on one side or the other of that issue; none were neutral. The civil rights movement was more visceral in the old, segregated south, than in the north. Two guys who've been under my skin my whole life, Blackie Damon and Andrew Vest. One a suspiciously swarthy doctor, the other a WASP, left-wing cleric who raised the issue of racial justice in the still segregated south. They were both your lovers, weren't they, Maggie?"

"I think you mean your lovers, Henry. Yes, they mattered to me. A lot. I think you had your own reasons for adopting them into your pantheon of heroes."

"Was Blackie's racial history common knowledge, Maggie? Or a carefully guarded secret? I mean, what did your friends make of his looks, his deep voice? His nickname can't have come from nowhere."

"Fascinating question, Henry, not only about him, but about the illusion of racial purity that can still make people like us squirm. Looking back, Charleston was a racial laboratory. You didn't have to dig very far beneath those aristocratic southern facades to find some complicated genetic histories. In those days Charleston gentry would have sooner committed treason than acknowledge a Sally Hemings in their family history.

"You could ask similar questions about our Cuban family. In shut-down, racially-charged societies one was never sure who knew what. The omerta racial code was as strong as in any mafia. Anything that challenged sacred cows—racial purity about the most explosive—never saw light. Hinting at it was to court social exile. Or worse."

Long silence.

"Maggie ... what *do* we know about racial mixing in our DNA?"

"We're talking about a lot more than Charleston in the 1940s, Henry. Or just *our* family. We provide a window into racial history more subtle than Barack Obama's, but no less volatile. Does it help you make sense of why it was that our family, establishment to our toenails, joined freedom movements, seemingly against our own interests? Is racial identity, conscious or not, such a huge reach? Cuba, Mexico, the United States, generation after generation, our forebears' solidarity with darker skin, poor people? There's never a single reason people throw over their comfortable lives, but there are reasons. Often hidden, forbidden secrets—racial, sexual. They have ways of, often unconsciously, motivating people to switch sides of the power divide.

"And, as you're discovering, choosing to exercise very different kinds of power."

Rather than unnerving, this was like opening a long-closed door, letting in fresh air.

"Oh my, Maggie, so maybe now you can connect the dots for me about Dr. Damon?"

Maggie snorted. "You're hopeless, Henry, this compulsion to connect dots. You and I, Jean, Victoria, Sylvia de Murias, Ben, Sarah Palmer—a lot of dots, all connected, but not by straight lines, forming a course no compass could chart. Yes, those of us who cared to, knew Blackie's nickname was more ironic than his father had any clue when he began calling him that as a very little boy.

"How many were prepared to consider the likelihood that Blackie's history was common, not unique, touching just about all of us? Charleston was not ready for that."

This was hardly the first time I'd wondered about the possibility of the blood of more than one race running in my veins. I'd figured Maggie's, not Ben's side. But like the sugar plantations Maggie's family had in Cuba, the Simpsons had plantations in the American south.

The blood in my veins felt thicker, warmer, richer.

"Alice and I have never had a conversation about this, Maggie. Such a powerful thing."

"Henry, you and Alice are legion. Except for unmistakably light-skinned people who marry unmistakably dark-skinned people, almost no one ever has this conversation. It's been buried so deep for so long, not only in this country, it rarely occurs to people there's any reason to."

"Fills gaps I didn't even know were there. And feels hugely welcome."

"That isn't the way everyone would feel, Henry. You know that."

I laughed. "You suggesting virtually the entire white western establishment is passing?"

"Served *you* pretty well for sixty years."

Before Alice came home, I began work on a poem the Maggie conversations had been building in me for several weeks.

Every So Often

Every so often
seldom
in an unguarded moment
I see the day's setup for what it is

a hedge
against the irreversible
inevitable

a new stick of deodorant in the
medicine cabinet behind the
old stick
that may well last longer

than I will

the same for toothpaste and
chocolate-covered espresso beans
not to mention
ibuprofen

why—you'd wonder if you were
unpacking my life
after the fact –
would he have hoarded more than he could ever have
enjoyed

in the time left

On our after-supper walk, I was unusually aware of Gabby's attention to squirrels, chipmunks, Canada geese high over-head, taking turns leading the V, barn swallows dive-bombing, scolding as we must have walked near their nests (territorial, like Alice and me). The owl hooting from the woods beneath the ridge. Kin everywhere, in ways I so often missed.

We took the cemetery route. I stopped at Minnie Stetson's pink stone marker. "Minnie, would it surprise you to know that someone with dark skin in their DNA was living in your house? How about you, or Hollis?"

"Thanks, Minnie, for not answering." One conversation from the dead was quite enough.

When we got home I sent my sisters an email.

From: Henry
To: Victoria
cc: Jean

Has it ever occurred to you that one possible explanation for our ongoing lefty views could be explained by mixed race in our DNA?

From: Jean
To: Henry
cc: Victoria

No, Henry, it hasn't. Not because I assume we're pure-breds. I don't think there is any such thing. I can't speak for

Victoria, but this doesn't grab me. What difference does it make?

From: Victoria
To: Henry
cc: Jean

Unless you're stuck back on that ridiculous purity thing, it's pretty insignificant, Henry, what our motives are. Everything we do is for such a mixture of reasons that the most clever shrink couldn't unpack them all.

From: Henry
To: Victoria
cc: Jean

OK, ladies. The big deal to me isn't only about motives, but whether there is identity hidden in us that longs to see light.

From: Jean
To: Henry
cc: Victoria

Let 'er rip, Henry. Can't say it grabs me the way it does you. If I was of an age to be considering another child, it might. Be kind of interesting, kind of cool, to have a recessive gene punch out a little pickaninny.

From: Victoria

To: Jean
cc: Henry

Jesus, Victoria, better hope the NSA doesn't read *that* one. *Pickaninny*? Talk about reverting to our politically incorrect, southern roots!

From: Henry
To: Jean
cc: Victoria

Do either of you remember Terry Robinson, the little girl Maggie befriended? She taught her to read, introduced her to some pretty sophisticated literature—got her reading *In Cold Blood* before she was twelve.

From: Victoria
To: Henry
cc: Jean

Was she the one Mom got to Johns Hopkins for a gender change? Black, yes?

From: Henry
To: Victoria
cc: Jean

Yes, but she was white—English—and after her gender change she married the family's black chauffer. The whole package. Color, gender, power, gives me a sense of why Maggie bonded with her.

From: Jean
To: Henry
cc: Victoria

You going to do the transgender thing next, Henry? I wondered what was in it for Mom to get that girl to Johns Hopkins. I thought it had to do with David Daniels, whom I'm pretty sure was her lover at one point.

From: Henry
To: Jean
cc: Victoria

Got it. Just one more thing you two seem to have been tuned into, that came as a surprise to me. Mine to massage.

From: Victoria
To: Henry
cc: Jean

You're on your own with this one, Henry. Am I fascinated by racial DNA we may have? Not really. You ever try that out on Alice? My guess is she'd tell you to go suck an egg.

⌣

"Alice," I said—violating the hard-learned lesson of waiting until she had gotten herself settled, coat off, briefcase in its place beside the desk, glass of wine poured—"would it shock you if it turned out the Simpson family has mixed race in our history?"

As she straightened up from putting down her briefcase, Alice gave me the long stare I'd seen her fix on an uncooperative witness. Then laughed.

"Oh Henry, you and your dead mother have been at it again. Mixed race? It wouldn't surprise me if you two decided that your ancestors mated with chimps at some point. How did you ever come up with this?"

Alice had that lawyer's way of making a serious suggestion seem absurd. As my sisters predicted. Their judgment, especially about women, is so much keener than mine.

"So you knew about the chimps? I'm so predictable, Alice; fascinated by ambiguity, especially about how I came to be me. Looking for clues for why I see the world the way I do."

"For that I can hardly blame you, Henry. Only my unquenchable love for you keeps me from considering you certifiable. You do have a unique take on the world. And on yourself."

That seemed to settle the matter for Alice, of considering dark-skinned DNA lingering in me, knitting together loose threads. So it seemed silly to Alice; so be it.

"I haven't done anything about dinner," I said, "hoped, if you aren't too tired, we might try that new French restaurant."

"Sounds dreamy, Henry."

At dinner, Alice poured out the twists and turns in the

day's depositions with her client, increasingly sure he'd been sandbagged in the cross-current between his firm and their secret relationship with the CIA.

"I don't know how closely you've been following the latest tapes Edward Snowden released, but in emails between the CIA and his firm is the smoking gun that will not only exonerate my client, but likely win him a huge settlement for their massive malfeasance."

No wonder an African in my ancestral woodpile was penny-ante to her.

"My goodness, Sweetheart," I said, as Alice ordered a glass of white to go with her flounder, "you're sure in the thick of what's-happening-now."

She smiled.

Over crème brulee—she allowed herself dessert only when ramped up by the day's events—she looked over at me, as if she had just noticed me. "That thing about you having dark-skinned DNA; were you being serious?"

She *had* heard. "Yeah, I was. The evidence is circumstantial, but compelling."

"That's an exciting thought," she said. I was eager for whatever would come next. "Henry, do you mind if we head home rather than have a cappuccino? I'm weary, and we're doing the rest of that deposition in the morning."

"I'm ready to go," I said.

Check race off the list of secrets needing to be dwelt on.

The next morning, after Gabby and I completed our obligations, I gave vent to the poem that had visited me during the night.

What Now, My Love?

I

Ego must die so
You
can live
my Love.

So you will do the
Work, Love,
Yes?

Excuse me, were you
speaking to me?
I felt myself
stiffen,   prepare to
resist,
sure signal that I feel
under assault.

Defend, protect. Protect what?
Why, myself, my Love.
And what self am I
Protecting?
Why, my own myself?

To live my Love I
must
surrender self and, with

       Jesus
             Buddha
        Ghandi
               King and

Bob Dole,

sweep clean
wide spaces fit for
royalty.

II

So what now, my Love?

My body, and my
200K Volvo
have mushy shocks
that lean and groan into
turns
they'd only recently mastered
with elegant
ease.

The surrender tender, it seems, is being
sweetened.
Dreams of world-class achievement and
acclaim
diffused,
released to

Mother Mary
Teresa
Coretta Scott King.

It's getting plainer
no matter what
I do or
don't
the mileage will wear smooth the
tread and I will
wearily, willingly
alongside my valiant
Volvo,
dress up a
barren bone yard, with my
skeletal sculpture of
vaunted vintage.

III

Set me down easy,
Love.

The bees buzz about my ears.
Your invitation
echoes in my head, even while the temple's cooling,

my blood pooling in
elbows and heels.

Gehenna, eager ego's
resting place.
Scavenger dogs lick once longing
loins
Feral cur fulfilling failed fantasy.

What now, my Love?

10,000 X 10,000
aeons of effort turned
to dust.
In the dust the storm stirs
the simple solemn secret
the muddy Mother of all
Egos.

Race. Mud. Why the exhilaration the possibility rouses
in me?

Heading to the attic to complete Alice's charge. Leave
Maggie's book for a while.

On a roll now. Things I had been loathe to let go—once
promised to solve riddles—no longer seemed important to
hang onto. Parish Easter letters, medals from swim races,
a citation for our parish housing homeless. Sermons I was
sure would initiate revolution. Were the riddles solved or
maybe no longer riddles? In less than an hour the cardboard

box was empty. Only Maggie's book, on the trunk. I folded the box flat.

I carted the armload down the stairs, feeling accomplished, the attic cleanout project ready for Alice's inspection. Maybe sweep. Sweep an unfinished attic? Alice, would. Keeping Maggie's book closed is like quitting therapy. I missed her. Maybe I'd asked enough of her.

What the hell. I'm not throwing the book out. Maybe one day.

At the trash bin in the garage, rather than dumping my whole armload, I put the notebooks, papers, pictures down, sat on the step, and began looking, one by one, before consigning each piece to Gehenna. Who knows what treasure might be buried among them?

My handwriting on the cover of notebooks: *Vietnam; Civil Rights; Preaching 1968—RFK, MLK, Jr., Dems in Chicago; Newspaper columns; Women's Ordination; Jesus & Sex; Domination or Cooperation; Conflicts with Vestries, with Bishops; Dissent from Bush's portrayal of Sept. 11; 9/11, Iraq Invasion.*

My life. Don't do this, Henry. Don't open those notebooks. You'll still be sitting right here when Alice comes home, and you know how that will turn out. But, shit, I'm going to toss out this rich stuff? Get a grip, man. Three months with Maggie, winnowing the chaff. Whatever in it matters is now lodged in your bones.

Best of all, Maggie herself, your main mentor, rescued from the shadows where you consigned her for fear of diminishing yourself. She's rehabbed your picture of yourself. Maybe hang her portrait that's been gathering dust in the attic, the cheesy one that Filipino artist did from her photograph, in a place of honor in your study.

I gathered the notebooks into a pile, without opening a single one, threw them all into the bin.

Nothing short of fucking heroic, Henry! Bravo! I retraced my steps to make sure I hadn't dropped any old journals. Not doing *that* again.

⌒

After a lunch of a cut-up apple slathered in chunky peanut butter, Gabby and I took a walk. Lovely, bright, sunny day. Gabby sniffed every bush and post, but he stopped more often than usual, sat, stared off. I was aware he wasn't himself, but I was preoccupied by possible future conversations with Maggie.

Maybe more focus on Ben, the father I wanted to please?

Comforted me that Maggie loved Ben. Sort of surprised me. Yeah, she thought he could be an asshole, but she was grateful for him, his steadfastness, the loyalty to our family. Counted for more than what he lacked. Makes me glad I can admit I'm grateful for Alice's hard-headed, legal perspective. Even though it can make me nuts. Fills gaps in my world. Not just Ben incarnate, wanting to shut me down. And be grateful to her for putting up with at least equal share my eccentricities.

Am I surprised at how big a part Maggie's hard-headed agnosticism played in forming my theology, if theology isn't too grand a name for it? Honestly, not really.

Did she have affairs with Andrew Vest or David Daniels?

Blackie Damon? Or maybe near misses, like several I had? Christ, my adolescence lasted a long time. Maggie's helped me claim my adult, made my poetry flow. Measure of psyche's health.

When we returned, I gave Gabby his favorite bone, but he didn't seem much interested.

I'd been concerned because he was starting to behave as our last Norfolk had shortly before she died. I was counting on Gabby to outlast me. He settled himself on his cushion, but something about the way his head was didn't look quite right.

Have you any idea what huge, irreplaceable space you fill in our life?

I don't have another poem in me like the one I wrote when your predecessor was nearing her end. I don't have more grief like that to spare, Gabby. Do me the kindness of letting me check out ahead of you.

Allysum had made a couple of seemingly miraculous recoveries, that turned out to add only weeks to her life. I wrote the poem after her first collapse, hoping it would magically make her live forever.

I didn't think we could recover enough to ever consider another, but Gabby stole into our hearts with just a photo from the breeder. How many more times do we have to do this?

Terrier's Time

The spring sun finally burned through winter's fog, warm-
ing our
   walk.
The dog seemed perkier, wanting to go
longer
than she'd been going these past few months. Her
13 years have deafened her
slowed her step.

She spied the cookie lady
sprinted to her eagerly accepting her morning
offering.
When we returned she
hurried
up the back stairs for her reward for coming
home.
She noisily lapped water, then turned to
scour
the floor for the tiny treats
The first one disappeared into her
mouth
and as she unreeled her tongue to take the other treat she
collapsed
onto her side
motionless,
still as, well, as
death.

Alice dropped to the floor beside her and felt her
heart
beating
I laid my head flat next to hers could see her eyes
moving
She twitched once, seemed to see us, tried without success
to gain her feet
heaved a heavy sigh and
rose heavily
as if for
Easter
seeming solemn, slightly chagrined, surprised perhaps to
find herself with
us.

We've been abnormally
attentive
since, rubbing her stomach, telling her of our
boundless
love.
So far,
though you can tell she finds it all a little much,
embarrassing
this living beyond dying, she's humored us, willing to
walk
and eat her treats as if none of us had
noticed.

That very night, as if I'd had a premonition, revisiting

that poem, came the dreaded moment. It's not as if Gabby hadn't given us plenty of warning. But, again, we chose denial. After dinner, as I was cleaning up, Alice asked, "Where's Gabby? Haven't seen him for an hour?" We went looking, found him lying on his side in the downstairs bedroom, gasping for breath. I lay on the floor next to him, my head next to his. His eyes were glazed over, unseeing.

"He's in a coma."

"You sure?" Alice asked.

"Oh God, I wish I weren't."

"What do we do?"

"Lie down here with him, stroke him, tell him we love him."

A wet spot on the rug beneath him. Oh God, he's letting go. Then he did. He stretched, front and back paws fully extended, head lifted, as he did when he'd been lying still for a long time; I thought he was coming around. Then his head drooped and his body went limp. I felt his chest. Nothing. Put my face to his nose. Nothing.

"He's dead," I sobbed. Alice lay down beside me. We sobbed for what seemed forever until we were exhausted. I stroked him one last time, went to the garage, got the same box I'd brought down from the attic just that afternoon, taped it back together. Alice picked up his tiny body, folded a towel around him, and placed him carefully into the box.

We stood, helplessly, looking at his body, needing to be sure he didn't take another breath before we closed the lid.

"I wish it were me, not him," I said through my sobbing. I meant it. I'd had enough grief for one lifetime. Gabby, the most trustworthy friend I ever had.

Alice and I drank more than normal that night, snacked on a few crackers, and went to bed without bothering with a proper supper.

Neither of us slept much.

I asked Andrew Vest, when I was eight and my dog was run over, if dogs go to heaven. His furrowed brow, furrowed even more.

"Do you love Birdie?" He asked.

"Oh yes, I sure do," I answered through my tears.

"Love is what we are after everything else about us is gone. You and Birdie are together forever. When you go to heaven, there will be Birdie, right with you where he has always been. Where he will always be."

↤

The next morning, before we took Gabby's body to the vet to be cremated, Alice and I unwrapped his little body and took a last look. It was torture patting that stiff fur. We'd called ahead. I was struck by how much the vet had become like an undertaker, receiving us at the back door, out of sight of people in the waiting room with their live animals.

The vet was gentle with us, practiced at this, making cooing sounds, not words that would be useless, even offensive. We drove home in silence, except for an occasional sob. Exhausted.

We arrived home, could manage only a banana and a cup of tea for breakfast.

"I'm sure our appetites will come back soon enough," Alice said, "but I just don't feel like eating now."

"What do you want to do now?" I asked, hoping she might come up with something that would make things better.

"I'm going to work," she said. "I need something to divert me. Getting really pissed off at the asshole that's defending the government, is just what I need."

I envied her that.

After she left, I wandered the house aimlessly, like someone with dementia. I thought about putting away Gabby's dish and bed, but couldn't bring myself to do either.

Maybe Maggie can help. She's dead, she understands, she can reassure me.

I climbed the attic stairs, my legs felt leaden. Perched on the steamer trunk, I picked up Maggie's book. The box that used to be here had become Gabby's coffin. I opened the book, shifting position, hoping to gather energy for Maggie. She'd know about Gabby; she always knew what we were going through. I hoped I could do this without having to give away more grief. I wasn't sure I had any more in me.

The book open beside me, I waited. Silence. I sat for several minutes.

"Maggie, you here?"

Nothing. Heart thumping. A touch of panic. What's up, Maggie? You abandoning me?

Silence. I sat for perhaps fifteen minutes, calming myself, waiting, anticipating her voice. Panic, then anger, back to fear, on to despair. Sadness. The whole panoply of grief, as if she'd just died. I didn't remember feeling it this much when you died. Why now?

"OK, Maggie, when the computer won't boot up, first

rule, turn it off, wait a few seconds, turn it back on. That's what I'm going to do with your book. Not that you're a computer."

That ought to get a laugh. Silence. Closed the book, put it down beside me, counting off seconds—one thousand and one, one thousand and two... one thousand and ten.

Long, deep breath, rearranged myself into a more comfortable position, picked up the book, slowly opened it.

Nothing. Gabby and Maggie on the same day? Who'll listen?

Not here; she's not coming. Gone. Dead, remember Henry? Like Gabby. Gone. Finished. No more. I turned a few pages, those names that unlocked all those doors to places I'd been skirting. Lighting my darkness. Turned to D—where Maggie and I lingered longest, sparring, joking, weeping—page turned down, as if to mark it. I fingered the fold.

In the margin in a familiar hand:

Nunc Dimittis, my dear son: Lord, Now Lettest Thou Thy servants depart in peace; for mine eyes have seen Thy salvation.